TVSK ● IVORIES

The phrase "it's a classic" is much abused. Still there may be some appeal in the slant of the cap Overlook sets in publishing a list of books the editors at Overlook feel have continuing value, books usually dropped by other publishers because of "the realities of the marketplace." Overlook's Tusk Ivories aim to give these books a new life, recognizing that tastes, even in the area of so-called classics, are often time-bound and variable. The wheel comes around. Tusk Ivories begin with the hope that modest printings together with caring booksellers and reviewers will reestablish the books' presence and engender new interest.

As, almost certainly, American publishing has not been generous in offering readers books from the rest of the world, for the most part, Tusk Ivories will more than just a little represent fiction from European, Asian, and Latin American sources, but there will be of course some "lost" books from our own shores, too, books we think deserve new recognition and, with it, readers.

Mount Analogue

A Tale of Non-Euclidian and Symbolically
Authentic Mountaineering Adventures

René Daumal

Translated from the French by Carol Cosman
Introduction by Kathleen Ferrick Rosenblatt
Afterword by Véra Daumal

TVSK IVORIES

Published by The Overlook Press

This Tusk Ivories edition is first published in the United States in 2004 by
The Overlook Press, Peter Mayer Publishers, Inc.
Woodstock & New York

WOODSTOCK:
One Overlook Drive
Woodstock, NY 12498
www.overlookpress.com
[For individual orders, bulk and special sales, contact our Woodstock office]

NEW YORK:
141 Wooster Street
New York, NY 10012

A CIP record for this book is available from the Library of Congress

Book design and type formatting by Bernard Schleifer
Manufactured in Canada
1-58567-342-0
1 3 5 7 9 8 6 4 2

Contents

Mount Analogue

Non-Euclidian Mountain Climbing

Eternity

He who binds himself to a joy
Does the winged life destroy
But he who kisses the joy as it flies
Lives in eternity's sun rise

—WILLIAM BLAKE

Mount Analogue is generally considered René Daumal's masterpiece, for it combines his poetic gifts and philosophical accomplishments in a way that is both entertaining to read and profound to contemplate. It is a many-leveled symbolic allegory of man's escape from the prison of his robotic, egoistic self. At the same time, it is well-grounded in scientific data and the facts of our physical existence.

After conducting his readers on an adventure into the depths of human materialism and spiritual ignorance in his previous book *A Night of Serious Drinking*, Daumal turns our attention to the heights of self-knowledge. The catharsis of the contraction phase of Daumal's life, as depicted in *A Night of Serious Drinking*, is followed by the phase of expansion and hope in *Mount Analogue*, a book dedicated to Alexandre de Salzmann. Looking away from the lower depths of the

Counter-Heaven of *Le Contre-Ciel*, the peak of the holy mountain emerges out of the fog.

In a letter he described his passage from the drinking bout to the mountain, a place where the caterpillar could transform itself into a butterfly:

> After having described a chaotic, larval, illusory world, I undertook to speak of another world more real and coherent. It is a long *récit* about a group of people who realized that they were in prison and who realized that they had to renounce this prison (the drama being that they [we] are attached to it).[1]

The book is subtitled *A Novel of Symbolically Authentic Non-Euclidean Adventures in Mountain Climbing*. Jack Daumal relates that René first began serious mountain climbing in 1937. Jack was better trained professionally and was able to pass his knowledge on to his brother. He says that René was a natural in the mountains and a quick learner. They made many climbs together in the two years preceding the outbreak of World War II. In a 1987 interview that I conducted for *Parabola* magazine, Jack said that in 1939 to 1940, the doctors recommended mountain air for René but no more climbing due to his tuberculosis. That is when the idea of Mount Analogue crystallized. Now that he was stuck in the lower climes, he remembered his métier was that of a writer:

> If I couldn't scale the mountains, I would sing of them from below. Then I began to think seriously with the heaviness and awkwardness with which one jostles one's thought processes, when one has conquered one's body by conquering rock and ice. I will not speak about the mountain but through the mountain. With this mountain as language, I would speak of another mountain which is the path uniting the earth and heaven. I will speak of it, not in order to resign myself but to exhort myself.[2]

Daumal's real-life passion for the mountains allowed him to transpose to the page the *rasa* of his own experience. This serves as an analogy expressing Daumal's own experience of a seeker's initiation into the "Path" (*Dharma*). A more specific interpretation is that it is an allegory for Daumal's experience in the Gurdjieff Work. The leader of the group, Sogol, like Totochabo of *A Night of Serious Drinking*, is generally considered to be a character based on Alexandre de Salzmann or Gurdjieff himself.

The narrator recalls an article he had written on "The Symbolic Significance of the Mountain," and this gives Daumal the opportunity to discuss various interpretations of this symbol from the Old Testament, Egypt, Islam, Greece, and especially from India, drawing on Guénon's study of symbolism of the mountain. The narrator recounts:

> The substance of my article was that in the mythic tradition, the Mountain is the connection between Earth and Sky. Its highest summit touches the sphere of eternity, and its base branches out in manifold foothills into the world of mortals. It is the path by which humanity can raise itself to the divine and the divine reveal itself to humanity.[3]

Throughout the entire novel there will be an interpenetration of symbols and concrete reality. The Hindus were the first to describe this way of seeing the world. According to Jan Gonda, the author of *Vedic Literature*, Vedic authors were always convinced of the existence of a correlation between the visible and invisible world—ritual acts, natural phenomena, and phenomena of divine agency: "The hold that nature has over man comes from the unseen powers within it."[4] This explains the Vedic tendency to avoid unequivocalness for reasons of taboo. Ambiguities help to blend the two spheres together. Daumal's text is imbued with this same parallelism between the visible and the invisible—the trek, the characters, and obstacles are all symbolic of the blending of the lower and the higher. Guénon had devoted an entire book, *La Grande Triade* (*The Great Triad*), to exploring this symbology. According to him, the base of the mountain, earth (passive perfection—*prakriti*), is a symbol for personality, designated by the personage Arjuna, the anxious warrior hero of the *Mahabharata*. The peak of the mountain connects with heaven (active perfection—*purusha*) and is a symbol for the evolved spirit, designated by the god Krishna, Arjuna's counselor. This symbology is perfectly enacted in the course of Daumal's story.

Among the many references to myths, Daumal's narrator recalls "those obscure legends of the Vedas, in which the *soma*—the 'nectar' that is the 'seed of immortality'"—is said to reside in its luminous and subtle form 'within the mountain.' Now, based on this symbolism, he proposes the physical existence of the ultimate mountain, which must be inaccessible to ordinary human approaches. While existing earthly mountains, even the mighty Himalayas, have been demystified by the profane, he finds the mythic mountains also inadequate because they have no geographical existence. He feels that Mount Meru of the Hindus, lacking real physical coordinates, "can no longer preserve its persuasive meaning as the *path uniting Heaven and Earth.*" Accordingly, he believes in the material existence of Mount Analogue: "*its summit must be inaccessible but its base accessible to human beings as nature has made them. It must be unique and it must exist geographically.* The gateway to the invisible must be visible."[5]

With deliberate brushstrokes, Daumal sketches in the essential details of plot and character. One of France's most eminent literary critics, André Rousseau, in a lengthy chapter, "L'Avènement de René Daumal" ("The Accession of René Daumal") of his book *Littérature du XXIème siècle* (*Literature of the Twentieth Century*), recalls René's description of the effort involved in producing what he called *la Chose-a-dire* ("the Thing-to-say"). "The Thing-to-say appears then in the most intimate part of oneself, like an eternal certainty."[6] Rousseau felt that there was not a single line in *Mount Analogue* where *la Chose-a-dire* does not hit us. Immediately, the proposed mountain-climbing expedition becomes intertwined with a quest for knowledge. The narrator and his soon-to-be-teacher, Sogol, are kindred souls, discovering each other in a manner reminiscent of Breton's "objective chance," that is, finding a kindred soul in an anonymous way—in response to an article. Here we see the synchronicity that will occur many times throughout *Mount Analogue*, the randomness and hidden order that surrounds us. Their chance encounter is also reminiscent of Daumal's lines in his essay "Nerval Le Nyctalope": "I was thus being observed! I was not alone in the world! This world which I had thought was only my fantasy!"[7] Contrast this with Sogol's note to the narrator: "Monsieur, I have read your article on Mount Analogue. Until now I thought I was the only person convinced of its existence," and the narrator's surprise: "And here was someone taking me literally! And talking about lauching an expedition! A madman? A practical joker? But what about me?"[8]

The teacher/seeker figure, Pierre Sogol, "with the tranquility of a caged panther," is a character drawn larger than life, who combines "a vigorous maturity and childlike freshness"[9] His thinking is described as being

> like a force as palpable as heat, light, or wind. This force seemed to be an exceptional faculty for seeing ideas as external facts and establishing new connections between what seemed to be utterly disparate ideas. [He would] treat human history as a problem in descriptive geometry . . . the properties of numbers as if he were dealing with zoological species . . . [and illustrate how] language derived its laws from celestial mechanics.[10]

Sogol's varied background recalls both de Salzmann and Gurdjieff, each of whom had many areas of expertise. The seeds of this charac-

ter were sown   back in 1934 when René was sent to collect de
Salzmann's material effects at the Hotel Jacob in Paris after his death
in Switzerland on May 3, 1934. He described the experience in a letter to Véra:

> It was certainly sad to undo all these balls of string that he planned
> to unwind himself one day. And to find so many projects started.
> There were mostly books: algebra manuals, adventure novels, old his-
> tory books, dictionaries, some perhaps of value, but I felt it useless to
> take them except for three or four. There remains: pieces of wood,
> paint supplies, an ax, plus his papers—sketches, studies, projects,
> plans, etc., and a magi marionnette.[11]

When we meet the composite character Sogol, he is currently an
inventor and teacher of mountaineering, accepting students only if
they first scale his Parisian apartment building and enter through the
window.

The narrator accompanies Sogol through his laboratory, which he
calls his "park." They meander down a pebble path through plants and
shrubs, among which are dangling hundreds of little signs, "the whole
of which constituted a veritable encyclopedia of what we call human
knowledge, a diagram of a plant cell . . . the keys to Chinese writing
. . . musical phrases . . . maps, etc." The narrator finally realizes the
brilliant logic of this information path:

> All of us have a fairly extensive collection of such figures and inscrip-
> tions in our head; and we have the illusion that we are "thinking" the
> loftiest scientific and philosophical thoughts when, by chance, sev-
> eral of these cards are grouped in a way that is somewhat unusual but
> not excessively so . . . Here, all this material was visibly outside of us;
> we could not confuse it with ourselves. Like a garland strung from
> nails, we suspended our conversation from these little images, and

each of us saw the mechanisms of the other's mind and of his own with equal clarity.[12]

Here, and many times throughout the book we see Daumal's rejection of busy behavior, overintellectualizing, and his general preference for quality over quantity. This reflects Daumal's study of Guénon (especially his book *Quantity and Quality*), and the Hindu preference for being rather than information gathering. In Buddhist literature, the material world is often referred to as the "10,000 beings." Daumal loves to evoke this image by making long lists of things, both in his novels and in his poetry.

Sogol and the narrator bare their souls for thirteen pages of the first chapter, entitled "The Meeting." They each share their disinterest and apathy for "this monkey-cage frenzy which people so dramatically call life."[13] Sogol recounts that after having experienced almost every pleasure and disappointment, happiness, and suffering, he felt he had completed one cycle of existence. He joined a monastery where he applied himself to inventing instruments, which rather than making life easier, would rouse men out of their torpor. Two such examples were a pen for facile writers that spattered every five or ten minutes, and a tiny portable phonograph equipped with a hearing-aid-like earpiece that would cry out at the most unexpected moments: "Who do you think you are?"[14] With hilarious inventiveness, Daumal applies Gurdjieff's theory of "alarm clocks"—employing reminding factors and resistances, little tricks to wake ourselves up. It also harks back to the Lilliputians of *Gulliver's Travels* who wore elaborate flappers to keep themselves roused. Finally, Sogol then relates that he left the monastery, continuing always to question this "grown-up" existence:

Fearing that death I suffer every moment, the death of that voice which, out of the depths of my childhood, keeps asking, as your does: "Who am I?" . . . Whenever this voice does not speak—and it does not speak often—I am an empty carcass, a restless cadaver."[15]

The narrator relates similar existential anxieties from his own childhood, echoes of Daumal's early experience:

In the evenings in bed, with the light out, I tried to picture death, the "most nothing of all." In imagination I suppressed all the circumstances of my life and I felt gripped in ever tighter circles of panic. There was no longer any "I." What is it after all, "I"? . . . Then one night, a marvelous idea came to me: Instead of just submitting to this panic, I would try to observe it, to see where it is, what it is. I perceived then that it was connected to a contraction in my stomach, a little under my ribs, and also in my throat . . . I forced myself to unclench, to relax my stomach. The panic disappeared . . . when I tried again to think about death, instead of being gripped by the claws of panic I was filled by an entirely new feeling, whose name I did not know, something between mystery and hope.[16]

By the fifteenth page, Daumal has posed the question three times: Who are you? Or Who am I? Together the two characters agree that there must be an answer to this question, there must exist, according to Sogol,

men of a superior type, possessing the keys to all our mysteries. Somehow I could not regard this as a simple allegory, this idea of an invisible humanity within visible humanity. Experience has proven, I told myself, that a man can reach truth neither directly nor alone; an intermediary must exist—still human in certain respects yet surpassing humanity in others.[17]

This excerpt echoes Gurdjieff's belief in an "Inner Circle of Humanity," a group that maintains an inner sanctuary of esoteric knowledge and secretly mediates in human events. It also reflects Daumal's personal experience in his early years of having failed on his own to find what he was seeking. He thus shares with us his own fortune to have found three of these intermediaries in the persons of the de Salzmanns and Gurdjieff. For him this allegorical tale is less farfetched than it might appear. Just as Sogol suggests, Daumal would not take Mount Analogue "simply as an allegory."

In chapter 2, entitled "Suppositions," Sogol spends ten pages providing the scientific data, complete with diagrams, to explain the anomalous properties of Mount Analogue. Because of the invisible closed shell of curvature that surrounds the island, it remains protected from human detection, but not always, not everywhere, and not for everyone. At a certain moment and in a certain place, certain persons (those who know and have a real wish to do so) can enter. This phenomenon is a scientifically embellished metaphor for Gurdjieff's explanation of how esoteric knowledge is not truly hidden but simply imperceptible to those who are not seeking it. "The Sun has the property of uncurving the space which surrounds the island. At sunrise and at sunset it must in some fashion make a hole in the shell, and through this hole we shall enter!"[18] Sogol presents the potential of synchronicity; his logic convinces the group of interested candidates and they all declare themselves willing to make the unprecedented journey.

Daumal provides a biographical profile as well as an actual ink sketch of each crew member, possibly attempting to create each of the twelve archetypes of human beings, as delineated by Gurdjieff. The eight remaining crew members together seem to represent different aspects of a single being. Among them we find the American artist (Judith Pancake), the Russian linguist (Ivan Lipse, probably based on Lavastine), the Austrian brothers—scientist Hans and metaphysician Karl. Four others drop out, epitomizing the stumbling blocks on the path to enlightenment, One is caught up in the joyous dance of maya (illusion), another is trapped in the veil of self-pity, and the others are too full of worldly concerns to leave the dream they inhabit.

By chapter 3, Daumal puts this cast of characters to sea, realistically and metaphorically. "We were not at all cut out to be sailors. Some suffered from seasickness . . . The path of greatest desires often lies through the undesirable."[19] Finally, in chapter 4, by a kind of syncretism of logic and magic, the sailors manage to penetrate the impenetrable envelope of curved space by doing nothing except being ready. In the true spirit of nonaction, the spirit of the Bhagavad Gita, the sailors are pulled in by a higher force:

> a wind rose out of nowhere, or rather a sudden powerful breath drew us forward, space opened before us, an endless void, a horizontal gulf of air and water impossibly coiled in circles. The ship creaked in all its timbers and was hurled up a slope into the center of the abyss, and suddenly we were rocking gently in a vast, calm bay surrounded by land![20]

They land, and are welcomed as though they had been expected. When they try to answer Daumal's favorite question, "Who are you?" they realize that, with the guides (who are in an advanced state of evolution), "We knew henceforth that we could no longer pay the guides of Mount Analogue with words."[21] They gradually orient themselves, wondering why the port of arrival is called "Port O' Monkeys." The narrator muses, "this name evokes in me, not too pleasantly, my entire Western twentieth-century heritage—curious, mimicking, immodest, and agitated."[22] Looking out into the port, they view "Phoenician barques, triremes, galleys, caravels, schooners, two riverboats as well, and even an old mixed escort vessel from the last century."[23] The search for consciousness knows no barrier of time, culture, or age; all come as monkeys.

As they prepare to ascend the mountain, they get carried away with their research and analyses of the Asiatic origins of local myths, the peculiar optical conditions of the island's atmosphere, and endless linguistic, sociological, and religious aspects. Suddenly they are roused by their guide from these preoccupations ("dreams" in Daumal's words) and realize how their idle curiosity was holding them back from their primary goal.

> We knew that nasty owl of intellectual cupidity all too well, and each of us had his own owl to nail to the door, not to mention a few chattering magpies, strutting turkeys, billing and cooing turtle doves, and geese, fat geese! But all those birds were so anchored, grafted so deeply to our flesh that we could not extract them without tearing our guts out. We had to live with them a long time yet, suffer them, know them well, until they fell from us like scabs in a skin condition, fell by themselves as the organism regained its health; it is harmful to pull them off prematurely.[24]

Here again we see the same little creatures that we met in "The Holy War" and A *Night of Serious Drinking*—the same physical imagery of foibles and fretting "grafted to the flesh." Only now, in Daumal's maturity, he understands that they too play a role in the process of evolution. Each individual had to renounce his current activities to go off on the journey. Later they had to give up their alpinist gadgetry and exploratory instruments for simpler provisions, as they prepared themselves for the mountain ascent.

> We began to call one another by our first names . . . this small change was not a simple effect of intimacy. For we were beginning to shed our old personalities. Just as we were leaving our encumbering equipment on the coast, we were also preparing to leave behind the artist, the inventor, the doctor, the scholar, the literary man. Beneath their old disguises, men and women were already peaking out.[25]

This concept of removing the trappings of one's personality and penchants that Daumal alludes to from his earliest writings onward is a common theme to all great works about the spiritual quest. A Sufi tale relates how the little stream succeeds in crossing over the desert by evaporating and allowing itself to be carried by the wind (dying in order to be reborn). In *The Divine Comedy*, Dante uses a metaphor similar to Daumal's: "One climbs to the summit of Bismantua with only one's feet: but here one has to fly; I say, fly with light wings and the feathers of a great desire,"[26] and, of course, in the Gospel, it is written: "Except a kernel of wheat die, it bringeth forth no fruit."[27]

Finally, Father Sogol declares that he gives up "my general's helmet, which was a crown of thorns for the image I had of myself. In the untroubled depths of my memory of myself, a little child is awakening and makes the old man's mask sob."[28] Father Sogol was trying to become *sanskrita*, "one who remakes himself," one who has an interior being and measure for judging. Only then could the mysterious synchronicity occur: at that moment he discovers a "peradam," the precious curved crystal hidden in the slopes of Mount Analogue "with an index of refraction so close to that of air despite the crystal's great density, the unaccustomed eye barely perceives it."[29] The paradam was considered to be a miraculous material entity, a little bit of evidence that slips through from another dimension of reality. Only when Father Sogol humbled himself, could he detect the tiny peradam, the highest material reward of a seeker's sincerity on Mount Analogue. Truly, this was the quintessential philosopher's stone, representing the activation of true insight, the reconciling energy that can reconnect man's two disparate natures. Pierre Sogol, whose very name meant *Stone Word*, could now touch the material evidence of his inner work.

If there is any doubt about the meaning behind Daumal's allegory, he provides short variations to drive home his message. Woven into the narrative are two beautiful mythic tales, "The History of the Hollow Men and the Bitter Rose," based on an old folktale of the Ardennes, and the "Myth of the Sphere and the Tetrahedron." The first story is a poetic allegory about man's place in the universe. "The hollow-men live in the rock, they move around inside it like nomadic cave dwellers. In the ice they wander like bubbles in the shape of men. "[30] The four pages that follow give free rein to his vast store of imagery, and express his inklings of another reality concurrent with our usual one. "Others say that every living man has his hollow-man in the mountains, just as the sword has its sheath, and the foot its footprint, and that they will be united in death."[31]

He draws upon Gurdjieff's theory that the energy we expend, especially that of our thoughts and emotions, is always used, eaten up by something else in nature's chain (the biggest consumer being our moon). "They eat only emptiness, such as the shape of corpses, they get drunk on empty words, on all the empty speech we utter."[32]

Then follows the drama of the twin brothers Mo and Ho and their battle with the Hollow Men in their search for the elusive Bitter Rose: "Whoever eats it discovers that whenever he is about to tell a lie, out loud or only to himself, his tongue begins to burn."[33] Finally Mo and Ho are forced to inhabit the same body and become a composite being, "Moho." If they continue to evolve, they might even become a *homo* (a man). This transformation recalls the metamorphosis of the caterpillar in *A Night of Serious Drinking*. The tale of the Hollow Men is yet another vision quest—a story of a search for knowledge encapsulated in Daumal's larger one, both in the tradition of the grail and the holy mountain.

Here, as throughout *Mount Analogue*, Daumal combines a lightness of poetic imagery with a weightiness of thought reminiscent of the poetry of the most Eastern of our Western literary ancestors, the Greeks. One line will be light as air, likening the Bitter Rose to a swarm of butterflies. Another has a weight as if it were carved in stone: "The hollow-men cannot enter our world, but they can come up to the surface of things. Beware of the surface of things."[34]

In his imagery, Daumal achieves the Hindu ideal of *suavité* (liquidity) which Visvanatha likened to flowing liquid. The Vedic literary scholar, Jan Gonda, believes that the Hindus achieved this suavity through the use of concise, elliptical phraseology, and vocabulary that was nuanced, melodious, and dignified. Daumal's imagery is not only liquid, but limpid—the quality of light passing through liquid. Visvanatha called limpidity the "evidence" produced by fire and water, the interaction of ardor and flow. Gonda also points out that Vedic writers often made graphic references to natural phenomenon, and showed a keen power of observation and pictorial expression. Likewise, Daumal presents a poetic, nuanced vision of the natural world. Now that he had achieved a certain security of having found a "path," it seems that he was finally able to see the holy in earthly images as well, rather than often denouncing them as in his early poetry. It bespeaks of his sense of joy as he was preparing to leave the earth. He graphically details Mo's movements:

> Sometimes like a lizard and sometimes like a spider, he crawls up he high red rock walls, between the white snows and the blue-black sky. Swift little clouds envelop hime from time to time, then release him suddenly into the light. And there, just above him, he sees the Bitter-Rose, gleaming with colors that are beyond the seven colors of he rainbow.[35]

The second myth is a prose poem that was also included in a 1954 collection of Daumal's poetry entitled, "Black Poetry White Poetry." It is another creation myth, similar to his earlier poem, "The Keys of a Big Game," reflecting the Vedic myth of primordial man multiplying himself into all forms and species. As in the earlier poem, this growth is conceived in terms of contraction and expansion. "In the beginning, the Sphere and the Tetrahedron were united in a single unthinkable, unimaginable Form. Concentration and Expansion mysteriously united in a single Will."[36] Daumal describes the familiar theme of the One multiplying into the many that he had experienced in his drug-induced death experience:

> The Sphere became primordial man who, wishing to realize separately all his desires and possibilities, broke into pieces in the shape of all animal species and the men of today. Man received the light of understanding. He wanted to see his light and enjoy it in multiple shapes. He was driven out by the force of the Unity.[37]

The form of *Mount Analogue* is a first-person narrative written in an understated, documentary style. It is the same style that we find in a dozen of his letters written to Véra, Jack, Jean Paulhan, Renéville, and others, while in the mountains during the years 1937 to 1943. Comprising thirty-two pages, these letters give lyrical, firsthand accounts of life in the mountains and include his experiences with the hardy mountain people. He describes his mountaineering training and how he would climb every other day, until walking on horizontal land seemed a little strange:

> There is nothing quite like the mountains for teaching slowness and calmness; there are climbs which take an hour of absolute slowness: left foot, right hand, walking stick here, right foot, walking stick there, body weight left, left hand . . . and here nervousness would kill. Once on top, the body discovers its paradise, which is taking off one's shoes and drinking a mouthful of wine mixed with snow gathered along the way.[38]

His description of the *névé* or glacier snow in *Mount Analogue* is lifted right out of his epistolary description to Rolland de Renéville where he lists ten different kinds, such as "wheat snow," "diamond snow," and "carpet snow."[39] One ten-page letter to his brother Jack is so replete with technical, montagnard jargon, that Daumal included thirty-six explanatory footnotes. Likewise, the detail of *Mount Analogue* reflects his expert knowledge of the subject, yet he never overburdens the novel with excess technical jargon that would intrude on the main poetic thrust.

The lightness and lyrical quality, reminiscent of Vedic poetry, is especially present in those mountain letters. It is clear that, in spite of his tubercular condition, Daumal was in his element several thousand feet up: his natural humor bubbles up everywhere to celebrate the mountainscape. These qualities emerge in *Mount Analogue* in a particular pattern: the beginning chapters are pervaded by a subtle humor, the middle chapters become more technical and scientific, and the final chapters achieve a joyful lyricism and exaltation. This progression gives a certain dramatic momentum to the voyage and climb.

The overall taste (*rasa*) of the book would fall into the Hindu category of "marvel," as in *A Night of Serious Drinking*, for a sense of marvel and strangeness is intended, in a very matter-of-fact way, from the first page. Whenever a camera was used on Mount Analogue, nothing would appear on the developed film. Some of the flora of Port O'Monkeys include the incendiary *lycoperdon*, which would spontaneously ignite through intense fermentation, and the talking bush, whose fruit in the shape of resonant gourds could reproduce all the sounds of the human voice when rubbed by its own leaves. Yet the down-to-earth reporting makes the strange phenomena—such as herds of unicorns, seem absolutely plausible. The casual tone belies the weightiness of the ideas behind the bare facts of the allegory.

I munched a piece of biscuit. The donkey's tail chased a cloud of flies into my face. My companions were also pensive. All the same, there was something mysterious in the ease with which we had reached the continent of Mount Analogue; and then, we seem to have been expected.[40]

In this book Daumal presents, in a veiled manner, many aspects of the teacher-disciple relationship of the esoteric tradition and of the Gurdjieff Work in particular. One important concept is the linkage that exists between seekers. One can never advance farther up unless one prepares for those behind. In the narrative, the guides explain to Sogol's band that each passing group must leave their encampment stocked with provisions for the next caravan. When the party sees the distant white smoke from the group ahead, they feel a mutual support: "For from now on the path linked our fate to theirs, even if we should never meet. Bernard knew nothing about them."[41] In the notes that he made for future additions to the novel, he talks further about the traces left by one seeker for another, warning the climber not to leave traces of false starts and mistakes. "Answer to your fellow men for the traces you leave behind."[42]

All seekers are linked through a hierarchy of evolved souls such as "the high mountain guides." Everything happens through the unfolding of a divine plan. When they wonder how they came to land, "we came to understand later that this was not by chance, that the wind that had sucked us up and led us there was no natural and fortuitous wind but a deliberate blast."[43]

In the last paragraph of the notes, the narrator lists the many factors that contributed to their successful entry: their calculations, their efforts, and their renunciation of bodily comforts. "So it seemed to us. But later we knew that if we had been able to reach the foot of Mount Analogue, it was because the invisible doors of this invisible country had been open to us by those who guard them."[44]

The interpenetration of the symbolic and the concrete—of fiction, fantasy, and the actuality of Daumal's own experience of the Gurdjieff Work and even of mountain climbing—makes the novel a real manual for the aspiring seeker. It is an itinerary of Daumal's many paths, showing how they all come together in one.

Thus Daumal uses fiction to present another crucial aspect of the teacher-disciple relationship. According to Ouspensky, "The first and most important feature of groups is the fact that groups are not constituted according to the wish and choice of their members. Groups are constituted by the teacher, who selects types which, from the point of view of his aims, can be useful to one another."[45] Yet the teacher does not clear the same single path for all disciples. Each person must find his own with the help of the teacher. In a letter to Ribemont Dessaignes, he wrote:

> The first sentence of the *Tao Tei King* is: "a path that is a path already traced is not the Path." I told you that I have encountered in my life a true teaching. One of the signs of its truth for me is that he never proposes a path already traced. No, at each step, the whole problem is posed. Nothing is resolved for me, once and for all.[46]

The novel remained unfinished with only meager notes to indicate the direction in which it might have gone. In the postface added by his wife, Véra, she discusses the preparation for the successive encampments: "It is very likely that René Daumal would have explained what he meant by this work of preparation. The fact is that in his own life he was working hard to prepare many minds for the difficult voyage toward Mount Analogue."[47]

The novel is truly a new embodiment of the Hindu concept of the mountain being the point where Heaven and Earth meet. In *A Night of Serious Drinking*, Daumal suggests "madness and death" as two escape exits, while the entire *Mount Analogue* constitutes the diary of an escape through the unnameable third exit alluded to in the previous novel. It is the log of someone on his way, a record left behind for others to read and follow. His proposed final chapter was to be entitled "And You, What Are You Seeking?"

Daumal indicates the preliminary stages of a true path as depicted in many traditions, a practical method for perfecting one's life here on this planet. Thus *Mount Analogue* represents the culmination of Daumal's expansion as a poet and perfectly reflects the esoteric teachings of Hinduism and Gurdjieff, both literary and philosophical. This final work is the consummation of all his years of honing his craft and his soul, surrendering his ego in order to ascend the holy mountain.

NOTES

1. R. Daumal, letter to Renéville, *Hermès* 5 (1967): 93.

2. R. Daumal, quoted in Rosenblatt, "Interior Resonances: A Conversation with Jack Daumal," *Parabola*, p. 90.

3. R. Daumal, *Mount Analogue*, p. 31. R. Daumal, *Le Mont Analogue*, p. 15. (In subsequent references, page numbers in parentheses will refer to the French version.)

4. Jan Gonda, *Vedic Literature*, p. 43.

5. R. Daumal, *Mount Analogue*, p. 32; (= p. 18).

6. Andre Rousseau, "L'Avènenment de René Daumal," *Littérature du vingtième siècle*, p. 67.

7. R. Daumal, "Nerval the Nyctalope," *The Powers of the Word*, p. 38.

8. R. Daumal, *Mount Analogue*, p. 30, 32; (= pp. 14, 19).

9. Ibid., p. 36; (= p. 27).

10. Ibid., p. 36–7

11. R. Daumal, *Correspondance*, Vol. 3, p. 57.

12. R. Daumal, *Mount Analogue*, p. 36; (p. 34).

13. Ibid., p 40; (= p. 39).

14. Ibid., p. 39; (= p. 39).

15. Ibid., p. 42; (= p. 40).

16. Ibid., p. 41–2; (= p. 40).

17. Ibid., p. 43; (= p. 40).

18. Ibid., p. 56; (= p. 67).

19. Ibid., p. 65; (= p. 84).

20. Ibid., p. 78; (= p. 110).

21. Ibid., p. 79; (= p. 112).

22. Ibid., p. 79; (= p. 113).

23. Ibid., p. 80; (= p. 114).

24. Ibid., p. 87; (= p. 128–29).

25. Ibid., p. 90; (= p. 134).

26. Dante, *The Divine Comedy* 4, v. 27–29.

27. Gospel of John 12:24.

28. R. Daumal, *Mount Analogue*, p. 90; (p. 135).

29. Ibid., p. 81; (= p. 117).

30. Ibid., p. 72; (= p. 128).

31. Ibid., p. 73

32. Ibid., p. 72

33. Ibid., p. 73; (= p. 101).

34. Ibid., pp. 74; (= p. 103).

35. Ibid., p. 74

36. Ibid., p. 85

37. Ibid., p. 85

38. R. Daumal, "Lettres de la Montagne," *Argile*, p. 184.

39. Ibid., p. 192.

40. R. Daumal, *Mount Analogue*, p. 93; (= p. 141).

41. Ibid., p. 95; (= p. 144).

42. Ibid., p. 106; (= p. 163).

43. Ibid., p.79; (= p. 113).

44. Ibid., p. 114; (p. 175).

45. Ouspensky, *In Search of the Miraculous*, p. 222.

46. R. Daumal, letter to Dessaignes, in Sigoda, *René Daumal*, p. 233.

47. Véra Daumal, in *Mount Analogue*, additional notes, p. 118.

Mount Analogue

CHAPTER 1

In Which We Meet

*Something new in the author's life—Symbolic mountains—A serious reader
—Mountaineering in the Passage des Patriarches—Father Sogol—An
internal park and an external brain—The art of getting acquainted—
The man who turns ideas inside out—Confidences—A satanic monastery
—How the devil for the day led an ingenious monk into temptation—
The industrious Physics—Father Sogol's malady—A story about flies
—The fear of death—With a raging heart, a mind of steel—A mad project
reduced to a simple problem of triangulation—A psychological law*

Everything I am about to tell began with a scrap of unfamiliar handwriting on an envelope. On it was written my name and the address of the *Revue des Fossiles,* to which I contributed and through which the letter had tracked me down, yet those penned lines conveyed a shifting mix of violence and sweetness. Behind the questions I was forming in my mind about the sender and the possible contents of the message, a vague but powerful presentiment evoked in me an image of "a pebble in the mill-pond." And from deep inside me the confession rose like a bubble, that my life had become all too stagnant of late. When I opened the letter, I could not have told you whether it had the effect of a revitalizing breath of fresh air or a disagreeable miasma.

In apparently one seamless movement, the same swift and flowing hand had written the following:

Monsieur,

I have read your article on Mount Analogue. Until now I thought I was the only person convinced of its existence. Today there are two of us, tomorrow there will be ten, perhaps more, and we can launch the expedition. We must make contact as soon as possible. Call me when you are free at one of the numbers below. I expect to hear from you.

Pierre SOGOL,
37, Passage des Patriarches, Paris

(This was followed by five or six telephone numbers which I could call at different hours of the day.)

I had almost forgotten the article to which my correspondent referred, which had appeared nearly three months before, in the May issue of *Revue des Fossiles*.

Though flattered by this show of interest on the part of an unknown reader, I felt a certain discomfort at seeing a literary fantasy taken so seriously, almost tragically. Yes, it had intoxicated me at the time, but was now a rather distant, retreating memory.

I reread the article. It was a somewhat hasty survey of the symbolic significance of the mountain in ancient mythologies. The different branches of the symbolic had been my favorite study for a long time—I naively believed that I understood something about the subject; furthermore, as a mountaineer I had a passionate love of the mountains. The convergence of these two very different kinds of interest in the same subject, mountains, had colored certain passages of my article with a definite lyricism. (Such conjunctions, incongruous as they may seem, play a large part in the genesis of what is commonly called poetry. I offer this remark as a suggestion to critics and aestheticians attempting to shed light on the depths of this mysterious language.)

The substance of my article was that in the mythic tradition, the Mountain is the connection between Earth and Sky. Its highest summit touches the sphere of eternity, and its base branches out in manifold foothills into the world of mortals. It is the path by which humanity can raise itself to the divine and the divine reveal itself to humanity. The patriarchs and prophets of the Old Testament behold the Lord face to face on high places. We have Moses's Mount Sinai and Mount Nebo, and in the New Testament the Mount of Olives and Golgotha. I even found this old symbol of the mountain in the scientific pyramidal constructions of Egypt and Chaldea. Moving on to the Aryans, I recalled those obscure legends of the Vedas, in which the soma—the "nectar" that is the "seed of immortality"—is said to reside in its luminous and subtle form "within the mountain." In India, the Himalayas are the abode of Shiva and his wife "the Daughter of the Mountain," and of the "Mothers" of all worlds—just as in Greece the king of the gods held court on Mount Olympus. In fact, in Greek mythology I found the symbol completed by the story of the rebellion of the children of Earth who, with their terrestrial natures and terrestrial means, tried to scale Olympus and penetrate Heaven with their feet of clay. Was this not the same effort pursued by the builders of the Tower of Babel, who, without renouncing their varied personal ambitions, expected to reach the One Eternal Being? In China, it was the "Mountains of the Blessed," and the ancient sages instructed their disciples on the edge of a precipice . . .

After making this tour of the best known mythologies, I went on to general reflections on symbols, which I arranged in two classes: those subject only to the rule of "proportion," and those subject, in addition, to the rule of "scale." This distinction has often been made. I shall review it all the same. "Proportion" concerns relations between the dimensions of a structure, "scale" the relations between these dimensions and those of the human body. An equilateral triangle, symbol of the Trinity, has exactly the same value whatever its dimension; it has no "scale." By contrast, take an exact model of a cathedral only a few inches in height. By its shape and proportions this object will always transmit the intellectual meaning of the structure, even if certain details must be examined through a magnifying glass. But it will no longer produce anything like the same emotion, or the same attitudes; it will no longer be "to scale." And what defines the scale of the symbolic mountain par excellence—which I propose to call Mount Analogue—is its *inaccessibility by ordinary human means*. Now, Sinai, Nebo, and even Olympus have long since become what mountaineers call cow pastures; and even the highest peaks of the Himalayas are no longer considered inaccessible today. All these summits have thus lost their analogical power. The symbol has had to take refuge in entirely mythical mountains, such as Mount Meru of the Hindus. But if Mount Meru—to take one example—is no longer situated geographically, it can no longer preserve its persuasive meaning as the *path uniting Heaven and Earth*; it can still signify the center or axis of our planetary system, but no longer the means for man to gain entry to it.

"For a mountain to play the role of Mount Analogue," I concluded, "*its summit must be inaccessible, but its base accessible* to human beings as nature has made them. It must be *unique* and it must *exist geographically*. The gateway to the invisible must be visible."

This is what I wrote. Taken literally, my article did, indeed, suggest that I believed in the existence, somewhere on the surface of the globe, of a mountain much higher than Mount Everest, which was, to any so-called sensible person, an absurdity. And here was someone taking me literally! And talking to me about "launching an expedition"! A madman? A joker? But what about me? As the author of this article, I was suddenly struck by the thought that my readers might have the right to ask me the same question. So, am I a madman or a joker? Or simply a scribbler?—Well, I can admit now, even while asking myself these rather disagreeable questions, that deep down, in spite of everything, I felt *that some part of me firmly believed in the material reality of Mount Analogue*.

The next morning, I called one of the telephone numbers at the corresponding hour indicated in the letter. A feminine and impersonal voice assaulted me immediately, warning me that I had reached the "Eurhyne Laboratories" and asking me to whom I wished to speak. After several clicks, a man's voice came to my rescue:

"Ah! It's you? You're lucky the telephone doesn't transmit odors! Are you free on Sunday? . . . Then come to my place around eleven o'clock; we'll take a little walk in my park before lunch . . . What? Yes, of course, Passage des Patriarches, and then? . . . ah, the park? That's my laboratory; I thought you were a mountaineer . . . Yes? Okay! We're on, then? . . . See you Sunday!"

So, he is not a madman. A madman would not have an important position with a perfume company. A practical joker, then? That warm and resolute voice was not the voice of a prankster.

That was Thursday. Three days to wait, during which my colleagues found me very distracted.

Sunday morning, dodging tomatoes, slipping on banana skins, brushing past sweating housewives, I made my way to the Passage des Patriarches. I passed through a front entrance, questioned the 'soul of the corridors'—the concierge—and headed towards a door at the back of the courtyard. Before entering, I noticed a double rope hanging down from a small window on the sixth floor, along a bulging, crumbling wall. A pair of corduroy pants—as much as I could see in such detail at this distance—emerged from the window; they were tucked into stockings that, in turn, disappeared in flexible shoes. The person who culminated in this fashion managed, while holding on with one hand to the window ledge, managed to shift the two lengths of rope between his legs, then around his right thigh, then diagonally over his chest up to the left shoulder, then behind the collar of his short jacket, and finally down in front over his right shoulder, all this with one flick of the wrist; he grabbed the lines below with his right hand and the lines above with his left, pushed off from the wall with the bottom of his feet and, with torso erect and legs apart, he descended at the speed of one and a half meters per second, in that style that looks so good in photographs. He had hardly touched the ground when a second silhouette engaged in the same descent. Arriving at the spot where the old wall bulged, this new person was hit on the head by something like an old potato, which squashed on the pavement, while a voice trumpeted from above: "So you'll get used to falling rocks!" He arrived below, however, not too disconcerted, but failed to end his "*rappel de corde*" with the gesture that justifies this name and consists of pulling on one of the lines to collect the rope. The two men went off separately and crossed the entryway under the eyes of the concierge, who watched them go by with a disgusted look. I went on my way, climbed the four flights of service stairs, and found this information posted near a window:

Pierre SOGOL, mountaineering teacher. Lessons Thursdays and Sundays from 7-11 o'clock. *Means of access:* go out the window, take a ledge to the left, scale a chimney, steady yourself on a cornice, climb a slope of disintegrating schist, follow the ridge from north to south skirting around several gendarmes. And enter by the dormer window on the east side.

I bowed willingly to these fantasies, although the stairs continued to the sixth floor. The "ledge" was a narrow edge of the wall, the "chimney" a dark recess that needed only to be shut by the construction of an adjacent building to be called a court, the "slope of schist" an old slate roof, and the "gendarmes" some mitered and helmeted chimneys. I entered through the dormer window and found myself standing before the man himself. Fairly tall, thin and vigorous, with a large black moustache and rather crinkly hair, he had the serenity of a caged panther lying in wait; he looked at me with calm, dark eyes and extended his hand.

"You see what I must do to earn my daily bread," he said to me. "I would have liked to welcome you to better quarters . . ."

"I thought you worked at the perfume company."

"Not only. I also work for a manufacturer of household appliances, a gear company, a laboratory for insecticide products, and a photography business. In all of them I am involved in attempting inventions thought to be impossible. Until now I've managed, but since they say I can't do anything but invent absurdities, they don't pay me much. So, I give climbing lessons to wealthy young men who are tired of bridge and crossword puzzles. Make yourself comfortable and get acquainted with my garret."

It was in fact several attic rooms with the partitions knocked out to form a low-ceilinged workshop, lit and ventilated at one end by a vast glass window. Under the window was squeezed the typical materials of a physics-chemistry lab, and a pebble path wound through the studio, imitating the worst sort of mule track, lined with small trees and shrubs in pots or planters, grass plants, small conifers, dwarf palms, and rhododendrons. Along the path, stuck to the windows and hanging from the ceiling, so that free space was used to the maximum, hundreds of small placards were displayed. Each one bore a drawing, a photograph, or an inscription, and all of them together constituted a veritable encyclopedia of what we call "human knowledge." A diagram of a plant cell, Mendelieff's periodic table, the keys to Chinese writing, a cross section of the human heart, Lorentz's formulas of transformation, every planet and its characteristics, a series of fossilized horses, Mayan hieroglyphs, economic and demographic statistics, musical phrases, representatives of the major plant and animal families, crystal samples, the plan of the Great Pyramid, encephalograms, logical formulas, charts of all the sounds employed in all languages, geographical maps, genealogies—everything, in short, that might fill the brain of a Pico della Mirandola of the twentieth century.

Here and there stood jars, aquariums, and cages containing extravagant fauna. But my host did not let me linger to look at his holothurians, his calamary, his waterspiders, his termites, his anteaters, and his axolotls . . . He led me onto the path where the two of us could just stand shoulder to shoulder, and invited me to take a stroll around the laboratory. Thanks to a small cross draught and the odors of the dwarf conifers, one had the impression of climbing the hairpin turns of an endless mountain trail.

"You understand," Pierre Sogol said to me, "we have such grave matters to decide, with repercussions in all the smallest corners of our lives, yours and mine, that we can't pull something out of nothing without at least getting to know each other. Today we can walk together, talk, eat, be quiet together. Later, I think we shall have opportunities to act together, to suffer together—and all of this is necessary in order to 'get acquainted,' as they say."

Naturally, we talked about the mountains. He had explored all the highest known ranges on the planet, and I felt that with each of us at the end of a good rope we might that very day have launched on the maddest mountaineering adventures. Then the conversation jumped, slipped, and veered, and I understood the use he was making of those bits of cardboard that spread before us the knowledge of our century. All of us have a fairly extensive collection of such figures and inscriptions in our head; and we have the illusion that we are "thinking" the loftiest scientific and philosophic thoughts when, by chance, several of these cards are grouped in a way that is somewhat unusual but not excessively so. This can be the effect of air currents or simply by constant agitation, like the Brownian movement that agitates particles suspended in a liquid. Here, all this material was visibly outside of us; we could not confuse it with ourselves. Like a garland strung from nails, we suspended our conversation from these little images, and each of us saw the mechanisms of the other's mind and of his own with equal clarity.

In this man's way of thinking, and in his whole appearance, there was a singular mixture of vigorous maturity and childlike freshness. But above all, just as I was aware of his nervous and restless legs, I was aware of his thought like a force as palpable as heat, light, or wind.

This force seemed to be an exceptional faculty for seeing ideas as external facts and for establishing new connections between what seemed to be utterly disparate ideas. I heard him—I'd be prepared to say I even saw him—treat human history as a problem in descriptive geometry, then, a minute later, speak of the properties of numbers as if he were dealing with zoological species. The fusion and division of living cells became a particular case of logical reasoning, and language derived its laws from celestial mechanics.

I could hardly reply to him, and soon felt dizzy. He perceived this, and then began to tell me about his past life.

"While still young," he said, "I had known almost every pleasure and discomfort, all the happiness and all the suffering that can befall man as a social animal. Useless to give you the details: the repertory of possible events in human destinies is rather limited, and they are nearly always the same stories. I will tell you only that one day I found myself alone, all alone, fully convinced that I had completed one cycle of existence. I had traveled widely, studied the most esoteric sciences, learned more than ten trades. Life treated me a little the way an organism treats a foreign body: it was obviously trying either to enclose me or to expel me, and I myself thirsted for 'something else.' I thought I found this something else in religion. I entered a monastery. A curious monastery. What, where—it doesn't matter; you should know, however, that it belonged to an order that was, to say the least, heretical.

"There was, in particular, a very curious custom in the rule of the order. Every morning our Superior handed each man—there were about thirty of us—a piece of paper that had been folded twice. One of these pieces bore the inscription: TU HODIE, and the Superior alone knew who had received it. I really believe that on certain days all the pieces were blank, but since no one knew, the result—you will see—was the same. 'It's you today'—this meant that the brother so designated, unbeknownst to the others, would play the roll of Tempter for the day. I have witnessed, among certain small African tribes and other peoples some ghastly practices—human sacrifices, cannibal rites. But I have never encountered in any religious or magical sect a custom as cruel as this institution of the daily Tempter. Imagine thirty men, living a communal life, already half-crazed by the perpetual terror of sin, looking at one another with the obsessive thought that one of them, without knowing whom, is specially charged with testing their faith, their humility, and their charity. There you have a diabolical caricature of a great idea—the idea that in my fellow man as in myself, there is both a person to hate and a person to love.

"One thing proves to me the diabolical nature of this custom: not one of the monks had ever refused to play the role of Tempter. Not one, when the *tu hodie* was handed to him, had the slightest doubt that he was capable and worthy of playing such a part. The tempter was himself a victim of a monstrous temptation. As for me, I accepted this role of *agent provocateur* several times, obeying the order, and it is the most shameful memory of my life. I accepted until one day I understood the trap I had fallen into. Up to that moment I had always unmasked the Satan on duty. These unfortunates were so naïve! Always the same tricks, which they thought were so subtle, poor devils! All their cleverness consisted of playing on a few fundamental falsehoods, such as 'following the rules to the letter is good only for idiots who cannot grasp their spirit,' or 'alas, with my health I cannot attempt such exertions.'

"Once, however, the devil for the day managed to catch me. This time he was a cheerful strapping rough-hewn fellow, with a child's blue eyes. During our rest period, he moved over to me and said, 'I see that you've recognized me. There's no fooling you, you are really too observant. Besides, you don't need this game to know that temptation is all around us, or rather within us. But look at the unfathomable spinelessness of man: all the means he's been given to stay alert he uses, in the end, to ornament his sleep. We wear a hair shirt the way we would wear a monocle, we chant matins the way other people play golf. Ah, if only today's scientists, instead of endlessly inventing new ways to make life easier, would put their ingenuity into fabricating instruments to jog man out of his torpor! There are plenty of machine guns, but of course that would be overdoing it . . .'

"He spoke so well that on that very evening, with my brain on fire, I obtained from my Superior the authorization to occupy my leisure hours with inventions and fabrications of this kind. I immediately set to work inventing mind-boggling devices: a pen for overly fluent writers that spotted or splattered every five or ten minutes; a tiny portable phonograph, equipped with a listening device like those on hearing aids that conduct the sound through the bones and which would shout at you at the least likely moments, for example: 'Just who do you think you are?' There was a pneumatic cushion, which I called 'the soft pillow of doubt,' which deflated unexpectedly beneath the sleeper's head; a mirror whose curvature was carefully designed in such a way—that one gave me trouble!—that every human face was reflected in it as a pig's head; and many others. I was thus fully employed—to the extent that I no longer even recognized the daily tempters. They had fun encouraging me. Then one morning I received the *tu hodie*. The first brother I encountered was the big strapping fellow with the innocent blue eyes. He greeted me with a cruel smile that was like cold water in my face. I saw at once the childishness of my inventions and the baseness of the role I was expected to play. Breaking all the rules, I went to find the Superior and told him that I could no longer agree 'to play the devil.' He spoke to me with a gentle severity, perhaps sincere, perhaps professional. 'My son,' he concluded, I see that you possess *an incurable need to understand* which prevents you from staying in this house. We shall pray to God that He wishes to call you to Him by other paths. . . .'

"That evening I took the train for Paris. I had entered the monastery under the name of Brother Petrus. I left it with the sobriquet Father Sogol. I have kept this nickname. My religious companions had called me this because of a turn of mind they had noticed in me, which at the slightest prompting made me take exactly the opposite position to all proposed assertions, always invert cause and effect, principal and consequence, substance and chance. 'Sogol' is a rather childish and pretentious anagram, but I needed a name that sounded good; and it reminded me of a rule of thought that had served me well. Thanks to my scientific and technical knowledge, I soon found jobs in various laboratories and industrial enterprises. Gradually I readapted to the life of the 'century,' but only externally, it's true. Deep down I can't manage to become attached to this monkey-cage frenzy which people so dramatically call life."

A bell rang.

"Fine, my good Physics, fine!" cried Father Sogol to his servant/ housekeeper; and he explained to me: "Lunch is ready. Let's go then."

He led me off the path and, gesturing to all the contemporary human knowledge inscribed on the little rectangles before our eyes, he said, in a low voice:

"Bogus, all this, bogus. There is not a single one of these cards of which I can say: here is a truth, a small, sure, and certain truth. There are only mysteries or mistakes in all this; where the first end, the second begin."

We came to a small, totally white room where the table was set.

"Here, at least, something *relatively real*, if one can bring these two words together without setting off an explosion," he went on as we sat down facing each other across one of those country dishes in which all the seasonal vegetables weave their vapors around a piece of boiled animal. "Again my good Physics calls upon all her old Breton shrewdness to put on my table the elements of a meal that contains no barium sulfate, no gelatin, no boric acid, no sulfuric acid, no formaldehyde, or any of the other drugs used in contemporary industrial food production. A good *pot-au-feu*, after all, is worth more than a mendacious philosophy."

We ate in silence. My host did not feel obliged to chat while eating, and I greatly admired him for that. He had no fear of being silent when he had nothing to say, or of reflecting before speaking. In reporting our conversation now, I fear I have given the impression that he never stopped talking. In reality, his stories and his confidences were interspersed with long silences, and quite often I put in a word myself. I told him, in broad outline, about my life, but that is hardly worth repeating here; and as for the silences, how can silence be described in words? Only poetry can do that.

After the meal, we returned to the "park," under the large window, and we stretched out on carpets and leather cushions. This was a very simple way of making a low-ceilinged area more spacious. Physics silently brought the coffee, and Sogol resumed his remarks:

"That fills the stomach, but little else. With a bit of money in this prevailing civilization, one manages well enough to obtain the basic physical satisfactions. The rest is bogus. Bogus, ticks and tricks, that's our whole life, between the diaphragm and the cranium. My Superior was right: I suffer from an incurable need to understand. I do not want to die without understanding why I have lived. And you, have you ever been afraid of death?"

I rummaged among my memories in silence, among the deepest memories which had not yet been put into words. And I said, with some difficulty:

"Yes. Around the age of six I heard something about flies that sting people while they sleep. Someone had joked that 'when you wake up, you're dead.' This phrase haunted me. In the evenings in bed, with the light out, I tried to picture death to myself, the 'most nothing of all.' In imagination I suppressed all the circumstances of my life, and I felt gripped in ever tighter circles of panic. There was no longer any 'I'—What is it after all, 'I'? I was not able to grasp it, 'I' slipped from my thought like a fish from the hands of a blind man. I couldn't sleep. For three years, these nights of interrogation in the dark frequently returned. Then, one particular night, a marvelous idea came to me: instead of just submitting to this panic, I would try to observe it, to see where it is, what it is. I perceived then that it was connected to a contraction in my stomach, a little under my ribs, and also in my throat; I recall that I was subject to irregular heartbeats. I forced myself to unclench, to relax my stomach. The panic disappeared. In this state, when I tried to think again about death, instead of being gripped by the claws of panic I was filled by an entirely new feeling, whose name I did not know, something between mystery and hope . . ."

"And then you grew up, went to school, and began to philosophize, didn't you? We're all like that. It seems that around the age of adolescence, the inner life of the young human being is suddenly weakened, its natural courage neutered. His thought no longer dares to confront reality or mystery face to face, directly; but endeavors to regard them through the opinions of 'grown-ups,' through the books and courses of professors. Yet the small inner voice is not entirely extinguished, and sometimes it cries out when it can, whenever a jolt of existence loosens the gag. It cries out its question, but we immediately stifle it. Well, we already understand each other a little. I can tell you, then, that I am afraid of death. Not of what we *imagine* about death, for this fear is itself imaginary. Not of my death whose date will be recorded in the civic registers of the state. But of that death I suffer every moment, of the death of that voice which, out of the depths of my childhood keeps asking, as yours does: 'What am I?' and which everything within us and around us seems bent on stifling. When this voice does not speak—and it does not speak often!—I am an empty carcass, a restless cadaver. I am afraid that one day it will fall silent forever; or that it will wake up too late—as in your story of the flies: when you wake up, you're dead.

"And there you have it!" he said, almost violently. "I've told you the main thing. All the rest is details. I've waited for years to be able to say this to someone."

He sat down, and I saw that this man must have a mind of steel to resist the pressure of madness that was boiling up inside him. He was now fairly relaxed, and seemed relieved.

"My only good moments," he went on after changing position, "were when I took my hiking boots, my rucksack, and my ice axe to climb the mountains. I've never had very long vacations, but I've made the most of them. After ten or eleven months spent perfecting vacuum cleaners or synthetic perfumes, after a night on the train and a day's journey by bus, when I arrive at the first snowfields with my muscles still poisoned by the toxins of the city, I always weep like an idiot, feeling my head empty, my limbs drunk, and my heart open. A few days later, wedged into a crevasse or astride a ridge, I find myself again, I recognize in myself characters I had not seen since the year before. But they were always the same characters after all . . .

"Now, in my readings and in my travels I have heard, like you, about men of a superior type, possessing the keys to all our mysteries. Somehow I could not regard this as a simple allegory, this idea of an invisible humanity within visible humanity. Experience has proven, I told myself, that a man can reach truth neither directly nor alone; an intermediary must exist—still human in certain respects yet surpassing humanity in others. Somewhere on our Earth this superior humanity must exist, and it cannot be absolutely inaccessible. And so shouldn't all my efforts be devoted to discovering it? Even if, in spite of my certainty, I were the victim of a monstrous illusion, I would have nothing to lose in making the effort, for in any case, without this hope, all life is meaningless.

"But where to look? Where to begin? I had already traveled the world, stuck my nose everywhere, into all sorts of religious sects and mystical cults, but to each one it was always: maybe yes, maybe no. Why should I stake my life on this one rather than that one? You see, I had no touchstone. But the very fact that there are *two* of us changes everything; the task does not become *twice* as easy, no: from being impossible it becomes possible. It's as if, to measure the distance from a star to our planet, you gave me *one* known point on the surface of the globe: the calculus is impossible. Give me a second point, it becomes possible, because then I can construct the triangle."

This abrupt leap into geometry was typical of him. I don't know if I understood him very well, but there was some force working to convince me.

"Your article on Mount Analogue was illuminating to me," he continued. "This place exists. We both *know* it. Therefore we will discover it. Where? That's a matter of calculation. I promise you that in a few days I will have determined its geographical position within several degrees. And we are ready to leave immediately, aren't we?"

"Yes, but how? What route do we take, what mode of transport, how do we pay for it? And how long do we stay?"

"Those are just details. Besides, I'm sure we will not be alone. Two persons convince a third and that creates a snowball effect—although we'll have to deal with what people call their 'common sense,' poor creatures. It's the common sense of water to flow . . . as long as it is not set over a fire to boil or into an ice tray to freeze. So if there's no fire . . . we'll hammer the iron until it gets hot. Let's set the first meeting on Sunday, here. I have five or six good pals who will surely come. Of course, one of them is in England and two are in Switzerland, but they will be here. We've always agreed that we would never attempt major expeditions without one another. And as major expeditions go, this will be a major expedition if there ever was one."

"On my side," I said, "I also have a few people who might be able to join us."

"Invite them for four o'clock, but you should come earlier, around two. My calculations will certainly be ready . . . Well, do you have to leave me already? All right, here's the way out," he said, showing me the little window hung with the rappelling rope. "Only Physics uses the stairs. Good-bye!"

Wrapping myself in the rope, which smelled of grass and the stables, I was down below in a few moments.

With an odd, floating sensation, I found myself in the street, slipping on banana peels, dodging tomatoes, and brushing against the sweating housewives.

If on my way back from the Passage des Patriarches to my apartment near Saint-Germain-des-près I had thought of regarding myself as a transparent stranger, I might have been able to discover one of the laws that governs the behavior of "featherless bipeds unfit to conceive the number (pi)," according to the definition Father Sogol gave to the species to which he, you, and I belong. This law might be formulated as follows: resonance to the latest statements we've heard. The guides to Mount Analogue, who would later reveal it to me, called it simply *the chameleon law*. Father Sogol had really convinced me, and while he was speaking to me I was ready to follow him on his crazy expedition. But the closer I came to home, where I would find all my old habits again, I pictured to myself my office mates, my writer friends, and my best pals listening to the story of the astonishing meeting I'd just had. I imagined their sarcasm, their skepticism, their pity. I began to mistrust my naivete, my credulity . . . so that when I began to tell my wife about my meeting with Sogol, I surprised myself by using expressions such as: "a funny fellow . . . ," "a defrocked monk," "a crazy inventor," "an extravagant project" . . . And I was stupefied to hear her say, at the end of my story:

"Well, he's right. I'm going to start packing my trunk this evening. After all, there are not just two of you—we're already three!"

"So, you're really taking this seriously?"

"It's the first serious idea I've encountered in my life!"

And the power of the chameleon law is such that I reverted to thinking that Father Sogol's enterprise was, after all, entirely reasonable.

CHAPTER 2

In Which Suppositions
are Made

The following Sunday, at two in the afternoon, I brought my wife to
the "laboratory" in the *Passage des Patriarches*, and after half an hour,
we three formed a group for which nothing was now impossible.

Father Sogol had nearly finished his mysterious calculations, but
he was reserving his disclosure until later when all the guests would be
there. While waiting, we entertained ourselves by describing to each
other the people we had invited.

On my side, there were:

IVAN LAPSE, thirty-five to forty, Russian of Finnish origin, a
remarkable linguist. Especially remarkable among linguists because
he was capable of expressing himself orally or in writing with sim-
plicity, elegance, and accuracy in three or four different languages.

Author of *Les Langues des langues* [The Tongue of Tongues] and of a *Grammaire comparée des languages de gestes* [A Comparative Grammar of the Languages of Gestures]. A small, pale man, with an elongated, bald cranium fringed with black hair, with long, slanted dark eyes, an aquiline nose, a clean-shaven face, and a rather sad mouth. An excellent glacier climber, he had a weakness for high altitude bivouacs.

ALPHONSE CAMARD, French, fifty, a prolific and admired poet, bearded, barrel-chested, with a rather Verlainian lethargy, redeemed by a warm, attractive voice. A liver ailment prevented him from lengthy ascents, so he consoled himself by writing fine poems about the mountains.

EMILE GORGE, French, twenty-five, journalist, a sociable, persuasive type, passionate about music and choreography, on which he wrote cleverly. A virtuoso of *"rappel de corde,"* who preferred the descent to the climb. Small, oddly built, scrawny with a chubby face, thick lips, and no chin to speak of.

JUDITH PANCAKE, an American friend of my wife's, around thirty, a painter of mountain peaks. Moreover, she is the only real painter of mountain peaks that I know. She has truly understood that the view from a high peak does not fit into the same perceptual framework as a still life or an ordinary landscape. Her canvases admirably express the circular structure of space in the higher altitudes. She does not consider herself an "artist." She paints simply to "have souvenirs" of her climbs. But she does it in such a workmanlike way that her pictures, with their curved perspectives, are strikingly reminiscent of those frescoes in which the old religious painters tried to represent the concentric circles of the celestial worlds.

On Sogol's side, there were, according to his description:

ARTHUR BEAVER, between forty-five and fifty, physician; yachtsman and mountaineer, and of course English; knows the Latin names, behavior, and properties of all the animals and plants found in all the highest mountains on earth. Not really happy except at an

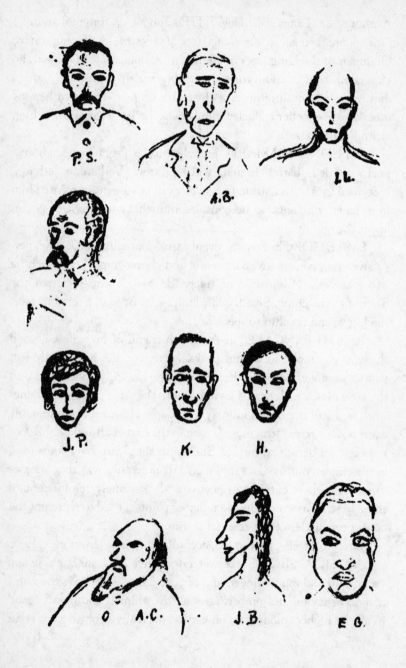

altitude above 15,000 feet. He forbade me from publishing in this account how long and with what equipment he had reached the summit of a particular peak in the Himalyas because, he said, "as a physician, a gentleman, and a true mountaineer, he avoided fame like the plague." He had a tall bony body, silvery blond hair paler than his tanned face, high, arching eyebrows, and lips poised delicately between naivete and irony.

HANS and KARL, two brothers—no one ever mentioned their family name—of around twenty-five and twenty-eight respectively, Austrian, specialists in acrobatic ascents. Both blond, but the first with an ovoid head, the second a rather square one; brilliantly fit with grips of steel and eagle eyes. Hans was studying mathematical physics and astronomy. Karl was interested chiefly in Eastern metaphysics.

Arthur Beaver, Hans, and Karl were the three friends Sogol had mentioned who formed, with him, an inseparable team.

JULIE BONASSE, between twenty-five and thirty, a Belgian actress. Just then she was having quite a successful career on the stage in Paris, Brussels, and Geneva. She was the confidante of a pack of young nobodies, whom she was guiding in the ways of the most sublime spirituality. She said, "I adore Ibsen" and "I adore chocolate eclairs" with the same tone of mouth-watering conviction. She believed in the existence of the "glacier fairy," and in winter she did a lot of skiing at the resorts where cable lifts take you up to the highest slopes.

BENITO CICORIA, around thirty, a ladies' tailor in Paris. Small, dapper, and a Hegelian. Although Italian by birth, he belonged to a school of mountaineering that might be roughly called the "German school." The method of this school might be summed up as follows: attack the steepest face of the mountain by the least favorable route subject to the greatest rock slides, and climb directly toward the summit, without looking to the right or the left for a more convenient way around. Usually you kill yourself, but from time to time a national party, roped together, reaches the summit alive.

B.C.

With Sogol, my wife, and myself, that made a dozen people.

The guests arrived more or less on time. I mean by this that since the meeting was set for four o'clock, Mr. Beaver was there first, at 3:59, and that Julie Bonasse, the last to arrive, delayed by a rehearsal, made her appearance just as the bells struck 4:30.

After the hubbub of introductions, we settled around a large trestle table and our host took the floor. He described the general outline of the conversation he had had with me, restated his conviction that Mount Analogue did indeed exist, and declared that he was going to organize an expedition to explore it.

"Most of you," he went on, "already know how I have been able to circumscribe the field of investigation in a first approximation. But two or three people are not yet up to date, and for them and also to refresh the memory of others, I shall go over my deductions again."

At this point he shot me a mischievous and meaningful glance, demanding my complicity in this clever lie. For no one, of course, was up to date. But by this simple ruse, each person had the impression that he was part of an ignorant minority, of being one of the "two or three who were not yet up to date," and, feeling the force of a convinced majority around them, hastened to be convinced himself. This method of Sogol's for "putting the audience in his pocket," as he later told me, was a simple application—he said—of the mathematical method that consists of "considering the problem solved"; or, jumping to chemistry, "an example of a chain reaction." But if this ruse was in the service of the truth, could it still be called a lie? In any case, everyone pricked up his ears.

"I shall sum up the premises," he said. "First, Mount Analogue must be much higher than the highest mountains presently known. Its summit must be inaccessible by means presently known. But second, its base must be accessible to us, and its lower slopes must be already inhabited by human beings like us, since it is the path that effectively links our present human domain to the upper regions. Inhabited, therefore habitable. Therefore presenting a set of conditions of climate, flora, fauna, cosmic influences of all sorts not so different from those of our continents. Since the mountain itself is extremely high, its base must be quite broad to sustain it: it must be an area at least as large as those of the largest islands on our planet—New Guinea, Borneo, Madagascar, perhaps even Australia.

"This said, three questions arise: How has this territory so far escaped the investigations of travelers? How do we gain access to it? And where is it?

"To begin with, I will answer the first question, which seems the most difficult to resolve. How could a mountain higher than all the peaks of the Himalayas really exist on our Earth without being detected? We know, though, *a priori*, by virtue of the laws of analogy, that it must exist. To explain why it has not yet been detected, several hypotheses come to mind. First, it might be found on the continent of the South Pole, which is still to some extent unknown. But mapping the points already reached on this continent and determining, by a simple geometric construction, the space that the human gaze could embrace from these points, we see that an elevation of more than 8,000 meters could not pass undetected—in this region or any other part of the planet."

This argument seemed to me, geographically speaking, rather debatable. But fortunately no one took up the gauntlet. He went on:

"Are we dealing with a subterranean mountain, then? Certain legends, told principally in Mongolia and Tibet, allude to a subterranean world, abode of the "King of the World," where traditional knowledge is preserved like an imperishable seed. But this realm does not correspond to the second condition of Mount Analogue; it could not offer a biological setting sufficiently akin to ours; and even if this subterranean world exists, it is likely to be found precisely beneath the slopes of Mount Analogue. All hypotheses of this kind being inadmissible, we are led to pose the problem differently. The territory in question must be able to exist *in any region* on the surface of the globe; therefore we must study under what conditions it remains inaccessible, not only to ships, airplanes or other vehicles, but even to the eye. I mean that it might be quite possible, *theoretically*, for it to exist *in the middle of this table* without our having the slightest inkling.

"To make myself understood, I will give you an analogous case."

He went into the next room to find a dish, put it on the table, and filled it with oil. He tore a piece of paper into tiny fragments, which he tossed onto the surface of the liquid.

"I have chosen oil because this highly viscous liquid will allow me to demonstrate my point more clearly than with water, for example. Let us assume that this oily surface is the surface of our planet. This bit of paper, a continent. This smaller piece, a ship. With the point of this needle, I gently push the ship towards the continent; you see that I never manage to get there. Within several millimeters of the shore, it seems to be repelled by a ring of oil that surrounds the continent. Of course, by pushing a little harder I manage to arrive. But if the superficial tension of the liquid were greater, you would see my boat circle around the continent without ever touching it. Now, suppose this invisible structure of oil around the continent repelled not only so-called 'material' bodies but light rays as well. The navigator on the ship continues to circle around the continent, not only without touching it but without even seeing it.

"This analogy is now too crude, so let's set it aside. You know, though, that any body does, in point of fact, exert a repulsive action of this kind on light rays that pass near it. This fact, theoretically foreseen by Einstein, was verified by the astronomers Eddington and Crommelin, on March 30, 1919, during an eclipse of the sun. They proved that a star is still visible, even when, in relation to us, it has already passed behind the solar disk. This deviation, no doubt, is tiny. But might there not exist unknown substances—unknown for this very reason—capable of creating around them a much more powerful *curvature of space?* This must be the case, for it is the only possible explanation of humanity's present ignorance of the existence of Mount Analogue.

"Here, then, is what I have established simply by eliminating all untenable hypotheses. Somewhere on Earth a territory at least several thousand kilometers in circumference must exist, where Mount Analogue rises. The base of this territory is formed of materials that have the property of curving the space around them in such a way that the entire region is enclosed in a *shell* of curved space. Where do these materials come from? Are they extraterrestrial in origin? Do they come from the Earth's core regions, whose physical nature we know so little about that, according to the geologists, all we can say is that no substance can exist there that is either a solid, a liquid, or a gas? I don't know, but we shall find out sooner or later *on the spot.* What I can deduce, however, is that this shell cannot be completely closed; it must be open above to receive radiation of all kinds coming from astral bodies, which are necessary to the life of *ordinary men;* it must also encompass a considerable mass of the planet, and doubtless opens toward its center for similar reasons."

(He stood up to make a quick sketch on a blackboard.)

"Here is how we are able to represent this space schematically. The lines I'm making represent the path of the light rays; you see that these directional lines open out, as it were, into the sky, where they join the general space of our cosmos. This opening out must take place at such an altitude—much above the layer of our atmosphere—that we must not imagine entering the 'shell' from the top by airplane or balloon.

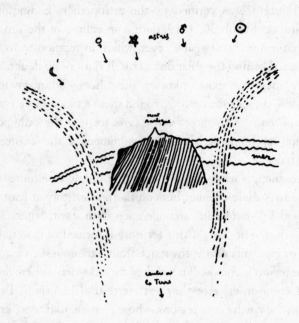

"Now, if we represent the territory on a horizontal plane, we have this schema. Mind you, the area around Mount Analogue must offer no perceptible spatial anomaly, since beings like us must be able to subsist there. We are dealing with a large, impenetrable *ring of curvature*, which surrounds the land at a certain distance with an invisible, intangible rampart—thanks to which, in short, *everything takes place as if Mount Analogue did not exist.* Supposing—I'll tell you why in a moment—the territory in question is an island, I would represent the path of a ship going from A to B like so. We are on this ship. The lighthouse is at B. From point A, I aim a telescope in the direction of the ship's progress; I see the lighthouse at B, whose light has bypassed Mount Analogue, and I will never suspect that between the lighthouse and me lies an island covered with high mountains. I follow on my course. The curvature of space deflects the light from the stars and also the lines of force of the terrestrial magnetic field, so although navigating with sextant and compass, I will always assume that I am going in a straight line. Without the rudder moving at all, my ship, curving itself along with everything on board, will hug the contour I have shown in the diagram A to B. So, this island might be as big as Australia, it is entirely understandable now that no one would ever suspect its existence. You see?"

Miss Pancake suddenly turned pale with joy.

"But that is the story of Merlin and his magic circle. I've always been convinced that the stupid business with Vivienne was invented after the fact by allegorists who missed the whole point. His very nature was to be hidden from our eyes inside his invisible circle, which could be just about anywhere."

Sogol was quiet for several moments to show that he very much appreciated this apt remark.

"Okay," Dr. Beaver said then, "but one day, surely, won't our captain notice that in order to go from A to B, he has consumed more fuel than he had foreseen?"

"Not at all—by following the curvature of space, the ship stretches out in proportion to this curvature; it's mathematics. The engines stretch, every piece of fuel stretches . . ."

"Oh, I understand! In effect, it all comes down to the same thing. But then, how shall we ever land on the island, supposing we could determine its geographical position?"

"That was the second question to resolve. I have tackled this by following the same methodological principal, which consists of assuming the problem solved and deducing from this solution all the consequences that flow logically from it. This method, I may tell you in passing, has always worked for me in every field.

"To find a way to reach the island, we must assume on principle, as we have always done, the possibility and even the *necessity* of doing so. The only admissible hypothesis is that the 'shell of curvature' that surrounds the island is not *absolutely* impenetrable—that is, *not always, everywhere,* and *for everyone.* At *a certain moment* and *a certain place, certain people* (those who know how and wish to do so) can enter. The privileged moment we seek must be determined by *a standard measure of time* common to Mount Analogue and the rest of the world; therefore by a natural clock, very likely the course of the Sun. This hypothesis is strongly supported by certain analogical considerations, and it is confirmed because it resolves another difficulty. Go back to my first diagram. You see that the lines of curvature are going to open out high up in space. How does the Sun in its diurnal course continually send radiation to the island? We are forced to conclude that the Sun has the property of 'uncurving' the space that surrounds the island. At sunrise and sunset it must in some fashion make a hole in the shell, and through this hole we shall enter!"

We all sat there stunned by the audacity and logical force of this deduction. Everyone was quiet, and everyone was convinced.

"There are, however," Sogol went on, "a few *theoretical* points that are still obscure; I cannot say that I understand perfectly the relation between the sun and Mount Analogue. But *practically,* there is no doubt. All we have to do is position ourselves to the east or the west of Mount Analogue (exactly east or west, if it is the moment of a solstice), and wait for sunrise or sunset. Then, for a few minutes—while the solar disk is still on the horizon—the door will open and, I repeat, we shall enter.

"It's already late. Another day I will explain to you (during the crossing, perhaps) why it is possible to enter from the west and not from the east: both for a symbolic reason and because of the air current. We still have the task of examining the third question: Where is the island situated?

"Let's continue to follow the same method. A mass of heavy materials like Mount Analogue and its substructure ought to provoke perceptible anomalies in the planet's movements—more serious, according to my calculations, than the few anomalies observed to date. Yet this mass exists. Therefore this invisible anomaly of the earth's surface must be compensated for by another anomaly. Now, we are lucky that this compensatory anomaly is visible; so visible even, that geologists and geographers have noted it for a long time. This is the bizarre distribution of dry land and sea which divides our globe into a 'hemisphere of lands' and a 'hemisphere of seas.'

He took a globe from a bookshelf and put it on the table.

"Here is the principle of my calculations. I first draw this parallel—between 50 and 52 degrees latitude north. This is the one that runs along the greatest length of dry land, across southern Canada, then across the Eurasian continent from southern England to Sakhalin Island. Now I draw the meridian that crosses the longest stretch of dry land. It is between 20 and 28 degrees longitude east and traverses the Old World approximately from Spitzbergen to South Africa. I leave this margin of 8 degrees because we can consider the Mediterranean either a true sea or simply a maritime enclave within the continent. According to certain traditions, this meridian should pass directly through the Great pyramid at Cheops. Well, the principle still applies. The junction of these two lines, you see, takes place somewhere in western Poland in the Ukraine or, in white Russia, within the quadrilateral Warsaw-Kracow-Minsk-Kiev . . ."

"Marvelous!" cried Cicoria, the Hegelian tailor. "I understand! As the unknown island surely has an area greater than this quadrilateral, the approximation is good enough. Mount Analogue is located, then, at the antipodes of this region, which puts it—just a minute, I'm making a few calculations—there: southeast of Tasmania and southwest of New Zealand, east of Aukland Island."

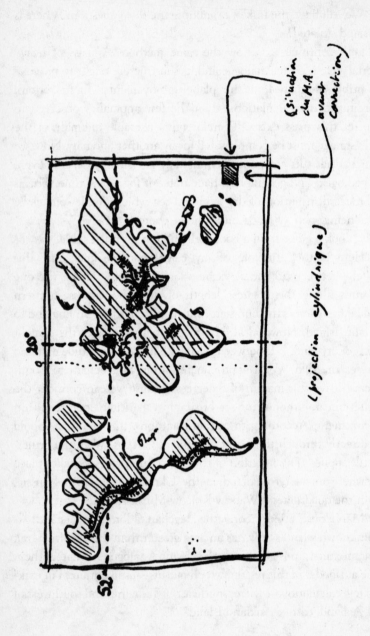

"Well argued," said Sogol, "well argued, but a little too hasty. This would be right if the dry lands had a uniform thickness. But let's suppose we cut out all the great continental masses on a planisphere in relief, and suspend the whole thing by a string hanging from the central quadrilateral. It is predictable that the great masses of the American, Eurasian, and African mountain ranges, almost all situated below the 50th parallel, will tilt the planisphere strongly toward the south. The weight of the Himalayas, the mountains of Mongolia and the African massifs will even outweigh the American ranges and shift the balance a little towards the east—but I'll know this only after more detailed calculations. Therefore, we must shift the center of gravity of the dry lands decidedly towards the south, and perhaps a little towards the east. This could lead us towards the Balkans, or even as far as Egypt, or towards Chaldea, the place of the Biblical Eden, but let us not presume . . . In any event, Mount Analogue remains in the South Pacific. I ask you for a few more days to refine my calculations. Then, we'll need some time for preparations—both to organize the expedition and to allow each of us to put his personal affairs in order for a long journey. I propose we set our departure for the first days of October; that leaves us two good months, and we would arrive in the South Pacific in November—in the spring.

"We still have to settle a number of secondary but important problems. For example, the material means of the expedition."

Arthur Beaver quickly intervened:

"My yacht *Impossible* is a good little ship, it has traveled around the world—she'll certainly take us there. As for the necessary funds, we'll see to that together, but from now on I'm certain we'll find what we need."

"For those good words, my dear Arthur," said Father Sogol, "you have the right to the title 'Redeemer of Millionaires.' Still, we have work to do. Each of us will have to do his share. Let's set our next meeting for next Sunday at two o'clock, if you all agree. I will tell you the result of my final calculations, and we'll devise a plan of action."

After that we drank a glass or two and smoked a cigarette, and by using the dormer window and the rope, everyone went on his own way, deep in thought.

Nothing much to report happened in the following week. Except for the arrival of a few letters. First of all, a little, melancholy note from the poet Alphonse Camard, who regretted that the state of his health, all things considered, did not permit him to accompany us. Still, he wanted to participate in the expedition in some way, and so he sent me several "Mountain Climbing Songs" thanks to which, he said, "his thought would follow us into this magnificent adventure." There were songs covering every mountaineering mood and circumstance. I shall quote the one I enjoyed most—although if you have never known the small miseries mentioned here, you will probably find it silly. It really is silly, but, as we say, it takes all kinds to make a world.

BALLAD OF THE LUCKLESS MOUNTAINEERS

The tea tastes like tin,
Twelve sleeping bags for thirty men,
They stay warm, it's true
But into the razor-sharp blue
Off they go at first light
Between black and white.

* * *

My watch has stopped, yours is off,
We're sticky with honey, the sky is all lumpy.
It's already daylight when we depart,
The snow patch is yellow before we start.
The pebbles are already raining down,
The cold has made our hands hang down.

There's gasoline in the drinking gourd,
And our fingers feel like gourds, as stiff
As a sweep's brush is the rope lift.

*   *   *

The hut was full of romping fleas,
The snoring defeated attempts at ease,
I'm getting frostbitten on my ear
And you look like a duck in gear.
I don't have enough usable pockets,
You found my compass among the plum pits.
My knife's forgotten but your toothbrush fits.

*   *   *

For twenty-five thousand hours we climb
And still we're stuck far down below,
The chocolate stopped us up but good,
We hack our way through the black ice flow
Like trying to wade around in cheese
Tasting bitter clouds, we cannot see
More than two steps ahead.

*   *   *

We halt a while to rest a bit,
There's my rucksack frolicking about
Making my heart skip a beat,
It gambols off far down below
Where holes are turning green to black;
Gurglings and railways, ten thousand sacks
On the moraine, false sacks and true holes,
And big, dirt-encrusted boles;
Finally, here's my schaos, put your cereal on my back,
Let's exchange pits of prudence for prunes.

*   *   *

We're laughing helplessly at this bad verse,
Snorting into our beards at the worst,
The air is crackling with hail
Our teeth are chattering, our knees fail.
The rock ledge is impregnable,
My memory's blocked, my stomach's a knot,
And two fingers are swollen a delicate green.

* * *

No one ever saw the summit
Except on the sardine can;
We yanked and yanked on all the ropes
Spent a lifetime untangling the lines on the slopes.
We fell into pastures, a bovine's trough:

"Had a good climb?"
"Fine, Monsieur, but rough."

I received a letter from Emile Gorge, the journalist. He had promised to join a friend in the Oisans in August, and make a descent from the Central Peak of La Meije by the southern face (we know that a stone falling from this summit toward the south takes 5 or 6 seconds before touching the rock). Then he had a report to do in the Tyrol, but he did not want us to delay our departure on his account; moreover, since he was staying in Paris, he offered to place any stories of the journey we wanted to send him.

Sogol had received a very long and very moving, vibrant emotional missive from Julie Bonasse, torn between the desire to follow us and her devotion to her art—this was the cruelest sacrifice the jealous god of Theater had ever asked of her . . . and perhaps she should have rebelled, and followed her egotistical inclination. But what would then become of her poor dear little friends, whose suffering souls she had taken under her wing?

"What?" Sogol asked me after reading me this letter, "It doesn't bring tears to your eyes? Are you so hardened that your heart doesn't melt like a candle? I was so moved by the idea that she might still be hesitating that I immediately wrote to encourage her to stay with her souls and her sublimities."

Finally, Benito Cicoria had also written. A deeper examination of his letter, which was a dozen pages long, led us to the conclusion that he, too, had decided not to accompany us. His reasons were presented in a series of truly architectural "dialectical triads." Impossible to summarize; for this we would have to follow his entire construction, and that would be a dangerous exercise. I will cite a line at random: "While the triad possible-impossible-adventure might be regarded as immediately phenomenizable and therefore as phenomenizing in relation to the first ontological triad, it is so only on the condition—frankly, epistemological—of a dialectical *reversus* whose prediscursive contents is nothing but a *prise de position historique* implying the practical reversibility of the ontologically oriented process—an implication which only the *facts* can justify." Certainly, certainly.

In brief, four wet blankets, as the popular expression goes. Eight of us remained. Sogol confided to me that he had expected some to quit. It was for that very reason that he had claimed, at our big meeting, that his calculations were not yet complete, when in fact they were. He did not want the exact geographical position of Mount Analogue to be known outside the members of the expedition. We shall see later that these precautions were in order, and even inadequate. If everything had gone precisely according to Sogol's deductions, if one element of the problem had escaped him, this inadequacy of precautions could have ended in disaster.

CHAPTER 3

In Which We Make
the Crossing

The following October tenth, we embarked aboard the *Impossible*.
There were eight of us, remember: Arthur Beaver, owner of the yacht;
Pierre Sogol, leader of the expedition; Ivan Lapse, the linguist; the
brothers Hans and Karl; Judith Pancake, the high altitude painter; my
wife, and myself. We had agreed not to tell our respective friends the
precise goal of our expedition; for either they would have thought we
were crazy, or more likely they would have believed we were making
up nonsense to conceal the true purpose of our enterprise, and that
might have generated all sorts of speculations. We had announced
that we were going to explore a few islands in Oceania, the mountains
of Borneo, and the Australian Alps. Everyone had made arrangements
for a long absence from Europe.

Arthur Beaver had the good grace to warn his crew that the
expedition would be long and possibly risky. He discharged and

compensated those of his men who had wives and children, and kept only three roughnecks, not counting the "Captain," an Irishman and an excellent navigator for whom the *Impossible* had become a second skin. We decided that the eight of us should replace the missing sailors, and anyway this would be the most interesting way to employ our time during the crossing.

We were not at all cut out to be sailors. Some suffered from sea-sickness. Others, who were never such masters of their bodies as when they were hanging over an abyss of icy rocks, could scarcely tolerate the little boat's long glides down the watery slopes. The path of greatest desires often lies through the undesirable.

The *Impossible*, with its two masts, sailed on whenever the wind was favorable. Hans and Karl managed to understand the air, the wind, and the sail with their bodies, just as they understood the rocky slopes and the rope. The two women worked all sorts of miracles in the galley. Father Sogol seconded the Captain, took our bearings, distributed tasks, helped us get our sea legs, and kept an eye on every detail. Arthur Beaver swabbed the deck and oversaw our health. Ivan Lapse taught himself mechanics, and I became a passable stoker.

The necessity of intense communal work bound us to one another as if we had been a single family, and a pretty unusual family we were. We formed an odd assortment of temperaments and personalities. To tell the truth, Ivan Lapse sometimes found that Miss Pancake hopelessly lacked any sense of the proper use of words. Hans eyed me skeptically whenever I ventured to talk about the "exact" sciences and thought my remarks disrespectful. Karl had trouble working with Sogol, who, according to him, smelled foul when he perspired. Dr. Beaver's satisfied expression every time he ate herring irritated me. But it was dear old Beaver who, in his capacity as physician and ship's master, was vigilant that no infection took hold in either the body or the psyche of the expedition. Whenever two of us began to get on each other's nerves, annoyed at the way the other walked, spoke, breathed, or ate, he always intervened at the right moment with gentle mockery,

If I were writing this story the way it might be written collectively, or the way each of us tells his own story to himself, noting only the most glorious moments in order to construct a continuous imaginary line, I would leave out these little details; and I would say that our eight hearts beat as one from morning to evening and from evening to morning with the same desire—or some such lie. But the fire that kindles desire and illuminates thought never burned for more than a few seconds at a time; in between, we tried to keep it in mind.

Happily, the difficulties of daily work, in which everyone played his vital role, reminded us that we were on this ship of our own free will, that we were indispensable to one another, and that we were on a ship, that is, a temporary habitation meant to transport us elsewhere; and if anyone forgot this, someone quickly reminded him.

In this regard, Father Sogol had told us that some years earlier he had made a few experiments meant to measure the power of human thought. I will report only what I grasped of this. At the time, I wondered if one should take all this literally, and always preoccupied with my favorite studies, I admired Sogol as an inventor of "abstract symbols"—an abstract thing symbolizing a concrete thing, contrary to custom. But since then, I have noticed that these notions of abstract and concrete have no great signification, as I should have learned by reading Xenophon of Elis, or even Shakespeare: a thing either is or is not. Well, Sogol had tried to "measure thought, not the way psychometricians and testing experts do, who only compare the way one individual performs this or that activity (often, moreover, entirely alien to thought) to the average performance of other individuals of the same age. Sogol's aim was to measure the power of thought as an absolute value.

"This power," said Sogol, "is arithmetical. In fact, all thought is a capacity to grasp the divisions of a whole. Now, numbers are nothing but the divisions of the unity, that is, *the divisions of absolutely any whole*. In myself and others, I began to observe how many numbers a man can really conceive, that is, how many he can represent to himself without breaking them up or jotting them down: how many successive consequences of a principle he can grasp at once, instantaneously; how many inclusions of species as kind; how many relations of cause and effect, of ends to means; and I never found a number higher than four. And yet, this number four corresponded to an exceptional mental effort, which I obtained only rarely. The thought of an idiot stopped at one, and the ordinary thought of most people goes up to two, sometimes three, very rarely to four. If you like, I will repeat several of these experiments with you. Follow me carefully."

In order to understand what follows, it is necessary to repeat the proposed experiments in all good faith. This requires a certain attention, patience, and mental calm.

He went on as follows:

"1) I dress to go out; 2) I go out to take the train; 3) I take the train to go to work; 4) I go to work to earn a living . . . Try adding a fifth link, and I am sure that one of the first three, at least, will vanish from your mind."

We did the experiment: he was right—and even a little too generous.

"Take another type of chain:

"1) The bulldog is a dog; 2) dogs are mammals; 3) mammals are vertebrates; 4) vertebrates are animals . . . I am going further: animals are living beings—but *voilà*, I've already forgotten the bulldog; if I remember the bulldog, I forget the vertebrates . . . In all orders of succession or logical divisions you notice the same phenomenon. That is why we constantly mistake accident for substance, effect for cause, means for ends, our ship for a permanent habitation, our body or our intellect for ourselves, and ourselves for something eternal."

* * *

The holds of the little ship were filled with various supplies and instruments. Beaver had studied the question of provisions not only methodically but inventively. Five tons of various foods were to be enough to keep all eight of us, plus the four crewmen, in good health for two years, without relying on any fresh food along the way. The art of nourishment is an important part of mountaineering, and the doctor had brought it to a high degree of perfection. Beaver had invented a "portable kitchen garden," weighing no more than five hundred grams; it was a mica box containing synthetic soil, in which he had planted certain extremely fast-growing seeds; every two days, on average, each of these devices produced a ration of green vegetables sufficient for one man—plus a few delicious mushrooms. He had also tried to employ modern methods of tissue culture (instead of raising cattle, he asked himself, why not raise steaks directly, but the results were merely heavy and fragile installations and revolting products, and he had given up these attempts. It was better to do without meat).

With Hans's help, Beaver had, on the other hand, perfected breathing and heating devices that had served him well in the Himalayas. The breathing device was very ingenious. A mask of elastic fabric was fitted to the face. The exhaled air was sent through a tube into the portable kitchen garden, where the chlorophyll of the young plants, superactivated by the ultra-violet radiation at high altitudes, separated from the carbon dioxide and provided the wearer with supplemental oxygen. The action of the lungs and the elasticity of the mask maintained a slight compression, and the device was regulated to ensure a high level of carbon dioxide in the exhaled air. The plants also absorbed the surplus of exhaled moisture, and the warmth of the breath activated their growth. Thus the animal-vegetable biological cycle functioned on the individual scale, which allowed a sensible economy of provisions. In short, we brought about a kind of artificial symbiosis between animal and vegetable. The other nourishing elements were concentrated in the form of flour, solidified oil, sugar, powdered milk, and cheese.

For very high altitudes, we were armed with oxygen tanks and the refined respiratory devices. I will speak in good time of the discussions stimulated by this equipment and its eventual fate.

Dr. Beaver had already invented clothes warmed by internal catalytic combustion, but after some experimentation, he had noticed that good down clothing with an inflatable lining conserved sufficient body heat to hike in the coldest climates. The heating devices were necessary only during bivouacs, and then we used the same heating apparatus used for cooking, fueled by napthalene. This highly transportable substance supplied a lot of heat in a small volume, provided it was burned in a special stove assuring complete (and consequently odorless) combustion. However, we did not know how high up our exploration would take us, and, ready for all contingencies, we had also brought outdoor clothing with double linings of platinum asbestos to be inflated by air filled with alcohol fumes.

Of course, we brought with us all the usual mountaineering gear: hiking boots and nails of all sorts, ropes, bolts, hammers, snap-links, ice axes, crampons, snowshoes, skis, and what have you, as well as observation instruments, compasses, clinometers, altimeters, barometers, thermometers, telemeters, alidades, photographic equipment, and other things. And weapons: guns, carbines, revolvers, cutlasses, dynamite, in short, whatever was needed to deal with any foreseeable obstacles.

Sogol kept the ship's log himself. I am too unfamiliar with maritime matters to discuss any incidents that might have effected the course of navigation; moreover, these were few and rather uninteresting. Sailing from La Rochelle, we put in at the Azores, at Guadelupe, at Colon, and after crossing the Panama Canal we sailed into the South Pacific during the first week in November.

It was on one of those days that Sogol explained to us why we had to try and approach the invisible continent from the west at sunset, and not from the east at sunrise. It was because at that moment, just as in Benjamin Franklin's experiment of the heated chamber, a current of cold sea air must rush towards the overheated lower levels of the atmosphere of Mount Analogue. Thus we would be sucked toward the interior; whereas at dawn, from the east, we would be violently repulsed. This result, furthermore, was symbolically predictable. Civilizations in their natural movement of degeneration move from east to west. To return to the sources, one should go in the opposite direction.

Arriving in the region that should have been located to the west of Mount Analogue, we had to proceed by trial and error. We were cruising at half speed, and just as the disk of the sun was about to touch the horizon, we steered towards the west and waited with baited breath, our eyes staring and tense, until the sun had disappeared. The sea was beautiful. But the wait was hard. Day after day passed this way, every evening bringing these few minutes of hope and skepticism. Doubt and impatience began to show their face aboard the *Impossible*. Happily, Sogol had warned us that these attempts by trial and error would take perhaps a month or two.

We held on. To pass the difficult hours after twilight, we often told stories.

I remember that one evening we talked about mountain legends. It seemed to me, I said, that the higher altitudes were more impoverished when it came to fantastic legends than the sea or the forest, for example. Karl explained it in this way:

"There is no place in the high altitudes," he said, "for the fantastic, because the reality itself is more marvelous than anything man could imagine. Could anyone dream of gnomes, giants, hydras, or catoblepas to compete with the power and mystery of a glacier, even the smallest glacier? For glaciers are living creatures, their substance renews itself by a constant periodic process. The glacier is an organized creature, with a head, its permanent snowpatch, which grazes on snow and swallows rocky debris, a head neatly separated from the rest of the body by the *rimaye*; then an enormous stomach in which snow is transformed into ice, a stomach furrowed by deep crevices and rivulets, which act as excretory canals for surplus water; and in its lower parts, it expels the waste from its food in the form of moraine. Its life has a seasonal rhythm. It sleeps in winter and awakens in spring with boomings and burstings. Certain glaciers even reproduce themselves, by processes that are scarcely more primitive than those of unicellular organisms, either by conjunction and fusion, or by rupture that gives birth to what we call regenerate glaciers."

"I suspect," Hans replied, "that this is a more metaphysical than scientific definition of life. Living beings are nourished by chemical processes, while the mass of the glacier is preserved only by physical and mechanical processes—freezing and fusion, compression and friction."

"Very well," answered Karl, "but you other scientists who study crystallizable viruses, for example, to find the transitional forms between the physical and the chemical and between the chemical and the biological, you could learn a lot from the observation of glaciers. Perhaps nature has made them in a first attempt to create living beings by exclusively physical processes."

"'Perhaps,'" said Hans. "'Perhaps' means nothing to me. What is certain is that the glacier contains no carbon, and consequently it is not an organic substance."

Ivan Lapse, who loved to display his knowledge of world literatures, interrupted:

"Nonetheless, Karl is right. Victor Hugo, returning from Rigi, which even in his day was not thought to be so high, noted that the views from the high peaks violently contradict our visual habits, that the natural there takes on the attractions of the supernatural. He even claimed that an average human mind cannot bear such a derangement of the senses, and uses this to explain the abundance of retarded individuals in the alpine regions."

"It's true, it's true, although this last theory is a howler," Arthur

Beaver spoke up. "Last evening Miss Pancake showed me some sketches of high altitude landscapes that confirm what you say . . ."

Miss Pancake spilled her cup of tea and squirmed awkwardly, while Beaver continued:

"But you are wrong when you say that the high altitudes are poor in legends. I've heard plenty of strange ones. Of course, I didn't hear them in Europe."

"We're all listening," Sogol prompted.

"Hold on," said Beaver. "I'd be quite happy to tell you one of these stories, though the people who told it to me made me promise not to reveal its source—but that's not important. I would like to tell it as accurately as possible, however, and to do that I'll have to reconstruct it in its original language, and our friend Lapse will have to help me translate it for you. Tomorrow afternoon, if you like, you'll hear it."

The next day, after lunch, the yacht was becalmed on a motionless sea, and we gathered to hear the story. Usually we spoke English together, sometimes French, for everyone knew both languages well enough. Ivan Lapse had preferred to translate the legend into French, and he read it aloud himself.

The Tale of the Hollow-men and the Bitter-Rose

The hollow-men live in the rock, they move around inside it like nomadic cave dwellers. In the ice they wander like bubbles in the shape of men. But they never venture out into the air, for the wind would carry them off.

They have houses in the rock with walls made of holes, and tents in the ice with canvas made of bubbles. During the day, they stay in the rock, and at night they amble onto the ice to dance in the full moon. But they never see the sun or they would burst.

They eat only emptiness, such as the shape of corpses, they get drunk on empty words, on all the empty speech we utter.

Some people say they have always existed and always will. Others say they are the dead. And still others say that every living man has his hollow-man in the mountains, just as the sword has its sheath, and the foot its footprint, and that they will be united in death.

In the village of A Hundred Houses lived the old priest-magician Kissé and his wife Hulé-Hulé. They had two sons, identical twins called Mo and Ho. Even their mother got them confused. To tell them apart, on their naming day the parents put a necklace hung with a little cross on Mo, and on Ho a necklace hung with a little ring.

Old Kissé had one great, unexpressed worry. According to custom, his eldest son should succeed him. But who was his eldest son? Did he even have an eldest son?

Reaching adolescence, Mo and Ho were already accomplished mountaineers. People called them *Passe-partout*. One day their father said to them: "To whichever of you brings me the Bitter-Rose, I will transmit the great knowledge."

The Bitter-Rose grew at the top of the highest peaks. Whoever eats it discovers that whenever he is about to tell a lie, out loud or only to himself, his tongue begins to burn. He can still tell lies, but then he is warned. Several people have seen the Bitter-Rose: from what they say, it resembles a kind of thick, multicolored lichen, or a swarm of butterflies. But no one has ever picked it, for the slightest trembling of fear nearby alarms it and it retreats into the rock. Now, even if a man desires it, he is always a little afraid of possessing it, and it promptly disappears.

In order to describe an impossible act or an absurd enterprise, they say, "It's like trying to see at night as though in broad daylight," or, "it's like wanting to turn on the sun to see more clearly," or even, "It's like trying to catch the Bitter-Rose."

Mo has taken his ropes, his hammer, his hatchet, and his iron hooks. The sun has surprised him on the flanks of the peak called

Hole-in-the- Clouds. Sometimes like a lizard and sometimes like a spider, he crawls up he high red rock walls, between the white snows and the blue-black sky. Swift little clouds envelop hime from time to time, then release him suddenly into the light. And there, just above him, he sees the Bitter-Rose, gleaming with colors that are beyond the seven colors of he rainbow. Over and over he repeats to himself the charm his father taught him that protects him from fear.

He ought to have a bolt here, with a stirrup of rope, in order to mount this horse of rearing rock. He strikes with his hammer, and his hand sinks into a hole. There is a hollow under the rock. He breaks the crust around it and sees that this hollow has the shape of a man: a torso, legs, arms, and hollows in the shape of fingers spread in terror; he has split the head with one hammer blow.

An icy wind blows over the rock. Mo has killed a hollow-man. He has shuddered, and the Bitter-Rose has retreated into the rock.

Mo climbs back down to the village and goes to tell his father: "I killed a hollow-man. But I saw the Bitter-Rose, and tomorrow I shall go to fetch it."

Old Kissé grew pensive. He could see the procession of misfortunes advancing from afar. He says: "Watch out for the hollow-men. They will avenge this death. They cannot enter our world. But they can come up to the surface of things. Beware of the surface of things."

At dawn the following day, Hulé-Hulé gave a great cry, stood up, and ran toward the mountain. At the foot of the red rock wall, Mo's clothing lay in a heap, and his ropes and his hammer, and his medal with the cross. His body was no longer there.

"Ho, my son!" she began to shout, "my son, they've killed your brother!"

Ho stands up, his teeth clenched, the skin of his scalp tightening. He takes his axe and wants to go. His father tells him: "First listen. Here is what you must do. The hollow-men have taken your brother.

They have changed him into a hollow-man. He will try to escape them. He will search for light at the seracs of the Clear Glacier. Put his medal around your neck along with yours. Approach him and hit him on the head. Enter into the form of his body. And Mo will live again among us. Do not be afraid to kill a dead man."

Ho looks as hard as he can into the blue ice of the Clear Glacier. Is it the light playing on the ice, do his eyes deceive him, or is he really seeing what he sees? He sees silver shapes with arms and legs, like greased underwater divers. And there is his brother Mo, his hollow shape fleeing from a thousand hollow-men in pursuit, but they are afraid of the light. Mo's shape flees toward the light, climbs into a great blue serac, and turns around as if searching for a door.

In spite of his blood curdling and his heart bursting—he tells his blood, he tells his heart: "Do not be afraid of a dead man"—he hits the head by cracking the ice. Mo's shape becomes motionless; Ho cracks the ice of the serac and slips into his brother's shape, like a sword into its sheath, like a foot into its footprint. He moves his elbows and shakes himself around, then pulls his legs from the mold of ice. And he hears words in a language he has never spoken. He feels that he is Ho and that he is Mo at the same time. All of Mo's memories have entered into his mind, along with the path up Hole-in-the-Clouds peak, and the place where the Bitter-Rose grows.

With the circle and the cross around his neck, he comes back to Hulé-Hulé: "Mother, you will have no more trouble telling us apart. Mo and Ho are in the same body, I am your only son Moho."

Old Kissé shed tears, his face unwrinkled. But there was one doubt he still wanted to dispel. He says to Moho: "You are my only son. Ho and Mo are no longer distinguishable."

But Moho tells him with conviction: "Now I can reach the Bitter-Rose. Mo knows the way, Ho knows the right move. If I master my fear I shall have the flower of discernment.

He gathered the flower, he received the knowledge, and old Kissé could leave this world in peace.

*   *   *

Once again that evening, the sun set without opening for us the door to another world.

Another question had much concerned us during those days of waiting. You do not go into a foreign country to acquire something without a certain amount of money. For bartering with prospective "savages" and "natives," explorers usually carry with them all sorts of junk and cheap goods—pocket knives, mirrors, knick-knacks from Paris, suspenders and stockings, trinkets, cretonne, bars of soap, *eau-de-vie*, old rifles, anodyne munitions, saccharin, *képis*, combs, tobacco, pipes, medals, and lots of cordage—not to speak of religious articles. As we might, in the course of the voyage and perhaps even in the interior of the continent, meet peoples belonging to ordinary humanity, we were provisioned with such merchandise as a means of exchange. But in our relations with the superior beings of Mount Analogue, what would constitute a trading currency? What did we possess that really had any value? What could we use to pay for the new knowledge we sought there? Were we going to beg? Or acquire on credit?

Each of us made a personal inventory, and each of us felt poorer from day to day, seeing nothing around us or in us that we could really call our own. In the end, we were just eight poor men and women, shorn of everything, watching the sun sink on the horizon.

CHAPTER 4

In Which We Arrive
and the Problem of Currency
Becomes Specific

Here we are—Everything new, no surprises—Interrogation—Settling in at Port-des-Singes—The Old ships—The Monetary system—The Peradam, standard of all value—The Forlorn inhabitants of the coast— Settling the colonies—Engrossing occupations—Metaphysics, sociology, linguistics—Flora, fauna and myths—Projects for exploration and study—"So when are you leaving?"—A Nasty owl—Unexpected rain— Simplifications in equipment, external and internal—The First Peradam!

A long wait for the unknown dampens the force of surprise. Here we are, settled for only three days in our little temporary house at Port-des-Singes, on the foothills of Mount Analogue, and everything is already familiar. From my window I see *The Impossible* at anchor in a cove, and a bay open onto a horizon similar to all marine horizons; only it rises perceptibly from morning to noon following the course of the sun, then sets from noon to evening through an optical phenomenon that Sogol, in the next room, is puzzling to understand. As I have been entrusted with keeping the expedition journal, I have been trying since dawn to set down on paper the story of our arrival on the Continent. I do not know how to capture that impression of something at once entirely extraordinary and entirely familiar, that staggering swiftness of *déjà-vu* . . . I have tried using my companions' personal notes, and certainly they are helpful. I was also counting to some extent on the photographs and films that Hans and Karl took; but when they were developed, no image appeared on the visible layer. It is impossible to photograph anything here with ordinary photographic material. Another problem for Sogol to puzzle out.

Three days ago, as the sun was once again about to slip under the horizon and we waited in the bow with our backs turned, a wind rose out of nowhere, or rather a sudden powerful breath drew us forward, space opened before us, an endless void, a horizontal gulf of air and water impossibly coiled in circles. The ship creaked in all its timbers and was hurled up a slope into the center of the abyss, and suddenly we were rocking gently in a vast, calm bay surrounded by land! The shore was so close that we could make out trees and houses, while above lay farms, forests, meadows, rocks, and, still higher up, the undefined ground and background of the high peaks and glaciers flaming red in the twilight. A flotilla of ten-man canoes—the rowers were certainly Europeans, their torsos naked and tanned—came out to tow us to an anchorage. It certainly seemed as though we were expected. The place strongly resembled a Mediterranean fishing village. We were not disoriented. The leader of the flotilla led us in silence to a white house, into a bare, red-tiled room, where a man in mountain dress received us on a carpet. He spoke French perfectly, but with the occasional secret smile of someone who finds quite odd the expressions he must use in order to make himself understood. He was translating, to be sure—unhesitatingly and correctly, but obviously translating.

He questioned us one after the other. Each of his questions, although quite simple—Who were we? Why had we come?—caught us off guard and shook us to the core. Who are you? Who am I? We could not answer him as we would a consular representative or a customs agent. Tell one's name and profession? What good would that do? But *who* are you? And *what* are you? The words we pronounced—we had no others—were lifeless, repugnant, and grotesque, like cadavers. We knew henceforth that we could no longer pay the guides of Mount Analogue with words. Sogol courageously took it upon himself to give them a brief account of our voyage.

The man who welcomed us was indeed a guide. All authority in this country is exercised by the mountain guides, who form a distinct class, and in addition to their strict profession as guides they take turns assuming the administrative functions indispensable in the coastal and foothill villages. He gave us the necessary information about the country and about what we were expected to do. We had landed in a small town on the coast populated by Europeans, for the most part French. There are no natives here. All the inhabitants have come from elsewhere, from the four corners of the earth, like us, and every nation has its little colony along the coast. How did it happen that we landed precisely at this town, called *Port-des-Singes* (Port of Monkeys), populated by Western Europeans like ourselves? We came to understand later that this was not by chance, that the wind that had sucked us up and led us there was no natural and fortuitous wind but a deliberate blast. And why the name Port-des-Singes, when there was not a single primate in the region? I'm not sure, but this name evokes in me, not too pleasantly, my entire Western twentieth-century heritage— curious, mimicking, immodest, and agitated. Our port of call could only be Port-des-Singes. From there we would have to reach the chalets at the Base on our own, two days' hiking in the high pastures, where we would meet the guide who could take us higher. So we would need to stay a few days in Port-des-Singes to prepare our supplies and put together a caravan of porters, for we would have to bring enough provisions to the Base for a very long stay. We were led to a very clean and sparsely furnished little house, where each of us had a kind of cell which he or she arranged to his liking, and there was a common room with a hearth, where we would gather for meals and for evening meetings.

Behind the house, a snowy peak peered at us from above its hunched shoulder. In front stood the port, where our ship lay at anchor, the latest in the strangest fleet ever seen. In the inlets along the shore, crafts from all epochs and countries were lined up in rows, the oldest encrusted with salt, algae, and barnacles making them almost unrecognizable. There were Phoenician barques, triremes, galleys, caravels, schooners, two riverboats as well, and even an old mixed escort vessel from the last century; but crafts of recent vintage were much less numerous. We could rarely identify the type or provenance of the oldest. And all the abandoned hulks were calmly awaiting petrification or digestion by marine flora and fauna, the dismemberment and dispersal of substance that are the final ends of all inert things, even those that have served the very greatest designs.

The first two days were chiefly spent transporting our cargo of provisions and goods from the yacht to the house, verifying the condition of everything, and beginning our preparation of the bundles that would have to be brought up to the chalets of the Base in stages involving several journeys. The eight of us did this all rather quickly, with the help of the "Captain" and three sailors.

The first stage would require a full day; there was a good trail, and we could use the large, agile donkeys native to the country. Later, everything would have to be carried on the backs of men. So we had to make arrangements for renting donkeys and hiring porters. The currency problem, which had so intensely preoccupied us, had been resolved, at least provisionally, upon our arrival. The guide who had received us had given us, as an advance, a sack of metal tokens that served here as a means of exchange for goods and services. As we had foreseen, none of our money had any value. Every new arrival or group of arrivals received this kind of advance to cover initial expenses, and one was committed to repay it during one's stay on the continent of Mount Analogue. But how could it be repaid? There are several ways, and since this question of currency and repayment is at the basis of all human existence and of all social life in the colonies along the coast, I must go into some detail on the subject.

One finds here, very rarely in the low lying areas, more frequently as one goes farther up, a clear and extremely hard stone that is spherical and varies in size—a kind of crystal, but a curved crystal, something extraordinary and unknown on the rest of the planet. Among the French of Port-des-Singes, it is called a *peradam*. Ivan Lapse remains puzzled by the formation and root meaning of this word. It may mean, according to him, "harder than diamond," and it is; or "father of the diamond," and they say that the diamond is in fact the product of the degeneration of the peradam by a sort of quartering of the circle or, more precisely, cubing of the sphere. Or again, the word may mean "Adam's stone," having some secret and profound connection to the original nature of man. The clarity of this stone is so great and its index of refraction so close to that of air that, despite the crystal's great density, the unaccustomed eye hardly perceives it. But to anyone who seeks it with sincere desire and true need, it reveals itself by its sudden sparkle, like that of dewdrops. The peradam is the only substance, the only material object whose value is recognized by the guides of Mount Analogue. Therefore, it is the standard of all currency, as gold is for us.

Truthfully, the only loyal and entirely satisfactory way of paying one's debt is to repay it in peradams. But the peradam is rare and difficult, even dangerous, to find and collect. Often one has to extract it from a fissure in the rock wall of a precipice, or pry it out from the icy edge of a crevasse. After efforts that sometimes last years, many people become discouraged and return to the coast, where they find easier ways to repay their debt. For this can simply be reimbursed in tokens, and these tokens can be earned by all the ordinary means. Some become farmers, others artisans, others stevedores, and so forth. We do not speak unkindly of them, for they make it possible to buy supplies on the spot, to rent donkeys and hire porters.

"And what if someone does not manage to pay his debt?" Arthur Beaver had asked.

"When you raise chicks," he was told, "You advance them the grain which, when they become hens, they will repay you in eggs.

But when a young hen doesn't lay when it matures, what becomes of it?"

And each of us had swallowed his saliva in silence.

This third day of our arrival, while I was jotting down these notes, while Judith Pancake was making some sketches on the doorstep and Sogol was racking his brains to solve difficult optical problems, the five others had gone off in different directions. My wife had gone for provisions, escorted by Hans and Karl, who on the way had become embroiled in a very complicated and confusing dialectical debate, it seems, on cruel metaphysical and para-mathematical questions. The issue was chiefly the curvature of time and of numbers: could there be an absolute limit to any enumeration of real and singular objects, after which one would suddenly find their unity again (said Hans) or their totality (said Karl)? In the end, they returned home quite heated and without noticing the kilos of foodstuffs they were carrying on their backs, consisting of fruits and vegetables, some familiar and others unknown to us. For the settlers had assimilated these from every continent, as well as dairy products, fish, and all sorts of fresh food so welcome after a long ocean voyage. The sack of tokens was large, we were not too scrupulous about the expense. And then, said Lapse, what will be will be.

Lapse himself had gone for a walk around the little town, chatting with everyone to study the speech and the social life of the place. He gave us a very interesting account, but what happened between us after lunch robs me of any desire to tell you about it. All the same, I will. I scarcely have the heart, but I'm not writing for my own amusement, and some of the details could be useful to you at this juncture.

The economic life in Port-des-Singes is quite simple, if lively, much like what it must have been in a small European town before industrialization; no thermodynamic or electric engine was admitted into the country, and indeed, any use of electricity was banned, which in a mountainous land rather surprised us. The use of explosives was also banned. The colony—mostly French, as I have said—has its churches, its city council, its police force. But all authority comes from above, that is, from the alpine guides whose delegates direct the administration and the municipal police. This authority is uncontested, for it is based on the possession of peradams. The people who have settled on the coast possess only tokens, which allow all purchases indispensable to the life of the body but confer no real power. Once again, let us not speak unkindly of these people who, discouraged by the difficulties of the ascent, have settled on the shore and the foothills, and make their small living there. Thanks to them, thanks to the initial effort they made to come this distance, their children at least do not have to make the voyage. They are born on the very shores of Mount Analogue, less subject to the nefarious influences of the degenerate cultures that flourish on our continents, in contact with the mountain men, and ready, if the desire takes them and their intelligence is awakened, to undertake the great journey from the place where their parents have given it up.

The majority of the town's population, however, seemed to have a different origin. They are the descendants of the crews—slaves, sailors of all epochs—from ships sailed to these shores throughout the centuries by seekers of the Mountain. This explained the abundance in the colony of foreign types in which one glimpsed the blood of African, Asiatic or even extinct races. Since women must have been rare among these crews of the past, one could only suppose that nature's harmonious laws had gradually reestablished the balance between the sexes by a compensatory preponderance of female births. In everything I set down here, of course, there are many suppositions.

According to Lapse's reports from the people of Port-des-Singes, life in the other colonies along the coast is quite similar to this: in each one every nation and every race has brought its own customs, costumes, and language. The languages, however, since the immemorial time of the first settlers and in spite of new contributions made by contemporary settlers, evolved in a particular fashion under the influence of the guides, who have special language. The French of Port-des-Singes, for example, presents many peculiar features, with archaisms, loan words, and also entirely new coinages to designate new objects, such as "per-adam." These peculiarities would be explained later as we came in contact with the language of the guides themselves.

Arthur Beaver, studying the flora and fauna of the region, returned all ruddy from a long walk in the nearby countryside. The temperate climate of Port-des-Singes favors the growth of plants and animals known in our countries, but unfamiliar species as well. Among these, the most curious are a tree-like bindweed, whose power of germination and growth is so great that it is used—like slow dyna-mite—to dislocate rocks for terracing work; the incendiary lycopodium, a fat puffball that bursts while casting out its mature spores, and then a few hours later suddenly catches fire by a process of intense fermen-tation; the rare talking bush, a sensory plant, whose fruits form sound boxes of various shapes capable of producing all the sounds of the human voice when rubbed by its own leaves, repeating like parrots the words pronounced in its vicinity; the hoop caterpillar, a multipede nearly two meters long that likes to curl up in a circle and roll at full speed from top to bottom of the rocky slopes; the cyclops-lizard, resembling a chameleon, but with a wide open frontal eye and two others that are atrophied, an animal commanding great respect even though it looks like an old scholar of heraldry. Finally, I must mention, among others, the aeronautic caterpillar, a kind of silkworm which in good weather produces light gases in its intestines and in a few hours inflates an enormous bubble that carries it into the air; it never reaches an adult state, and reproduces itself quite primitively by larval parthenogenesis.

Had these strange species been imported in distant times by set-tlers from the far reaches of the globe, or were they truly indigenous to the continent of Mount Analogue? Beaver could not yet settle the question. An old Breton, established as a carpenter at Port-des-Singes, had told and sung for him old myths—mingled, it seems, with foreign legends and teachings of the guides—that touched on the subject. The guides whom we questioned afterwards on the value of these myths always gave us what seemed to be evasive answers: "They are as true," one of them told us, "as your fairy tales and your scientific theories." "A knife," said another, "is neither true nor false, but anyone impaled on its blade is in error."

One of these myths conveyed this message in so many words:

In the beginning, the Sphere and the Tetrahedron were united in a single unthinkable, unimaginable Form. Concentration and Expansion mysteriously united in a single Will that desired only itself.

There was a separation, but the Unique remains unique.

The Sphere became primordial man who, wishing to realize separately all his desires and possibilities, broke into pieces in the shape of all animal species and the men of today.

The Tetrahedron became the primordial Plant, which similarly engendered all plants.

The Animal, closed to external space, hollowed himself out and developed lungs, intestines and other internal organs to receive nourishment, to preserve and perpetuate himself. The Plant, blossoming in external space, ramified externally to penetrate nourishment through roots and foliage.

Several of their descendants hesitated, or wanted to stay on both sides of the fence: these became the animal-plants that populate the seas.

Man received a breath, a light of understanding; he alone received this light. He wanted to see his light and to enjoy it in multiple shapes. He was driven out by the force of the Unity. He alone was driven out.

He went out to people the lands Out There, suffering, dividing against himself, multiplying out of the desire to see his own light and to enjoy it.

Sometimes a man submits in his heart, submits the visible to the power of light, seeks to return to his origin.

He seeks, he finds, he returns to his source.

The odd geological structure of the continent endowed it with the greatest variety of climates, and in three days' walk from Port-des-Singes one finds the tropical jungle in one direction and glacier terrain in the other, as well as steppes and sandy deserts. Each colony had been founded in the place most like the native land of its settlers.

For Beaver, all this was yet to be explored. Karl proposed to study the Asian origins he thought he detected in the myths Beaver had gathered. Hans and Sogol planned to install a little observatory on a nearby hill, where under the peculiar optical conditions of the country they would perform the standard measurements of parallaxes, angular distances, meridian passages, spectroscopy, and such, on the principal stars, to deduce precise notions about the anomalies caused in cosmic perspective by the shell of curved space surrounding Mount Analogue. Ivan Lapse continued to pursue his linguistic and sociological research. My wife was burning to study the religious life of the country, the modifications (and especially, she assumed, the purifications and enrichments) brought to the churches by the influence of Mount Analogue—whether in dogma, ethics, rites, liturgical music, architecture or the other religious arts. Miss Pancake would go into partnership with her in these last areas and especially those of the plastic arts, while pursuing her main work of documentary sketches, which had suddenly taken on considerable importance for the expedition since the failure of all photographic attempts. As for me, I hoped to draw precious elements from the diverse materials collected by my companions in order to advance my research on the symbolic. In so doing, however, I did not intend to neglect my main job, which was to keep the record of this expedition—the record that was later reduced to the account you are hearing now.

While giving ourselves over to these areas of research, we planned to profit from them to enlarge our stock of provisions, to do business perhaps—in short, we would not be wasting our time.

"So when are you leaving?" shouted a voice coming from the road one day, while we talked together about all these engrossing projects after lunch.

It was the guide delegated to Port-des-Singes who had interrupted us, and without waiting for an answer he continued on his way at that steady pace mountaineers have, scarcely seeming to move.

This woke us from our dreams. Thus, before even taking the first steps, we were slipping toward abandonment—yes, toward abandonment, for it was abandoning our goal and betraying our promise not to spend a single minute satisfying useless curiosity. Suddenly, our exploratory enthusiasms and the easy pretexts we'd parried seemed rather pathetic. We could hardly look at each other. We heard Sogol's voice growl under his breath:

"Let's nail this nasty owl to the door and leave without looking back!"

We knew that nasty owl of intellectual cupidity all too well, and each of us had his own owl to nail to the door, not to mention a few chattering magpies, strutting turkeys, billing and cooing turtle doves, and geese, fat geese! But all those birds were so anchored, grafted so deeply to our flesh that we could not extract them without tearing our guts out. We had to live with them a long time yet, suffer them, know them well, until they fell from us like scabs in a skin condition, fell by themselves as the organism regained its health; it is harmful to pull them off prematurely.

Our four crewmen were playing cards in the shade of a pine tree, and since none of them intended to scale the heights, their way of passing the time seemed reasonable. As they had to accompany us to the Base, however, and help us settle in there, we called on them to assist us in preparing for the departure, which we fixed for the following day, come what may.

Come what may . . . is easier said than done. The next morning, after we had worked hard all night to prepare the baggage, everything was ready, the donkeys and porters assembled, but it began to pour. It rained all afternoon, all night, it rained the next day, it rained buckets for five days. The roads were washed out, surely impassable, we were told.

We had to make use of this delay. First, we rethought the necessity of our material goods. All kinds of observational and measuring instruments, which had seemed to us more precious than anything, now seemed laughable—especially after our unfortunate photographic experiments—and several proved utterly useless. The batteries of our electric lamps did not work. They would have to be replaced by lanterns. In this way we got rid of a great many encumbering objects, which allowed us to carry more necessary provisions.

So we scoured the area to purchase supplementary food, lanterns, and local clothing. These, although very simple, were much superior to ours, the result of the settlers' long experience. At specialty shops we found all sorts of dried and preserved food that would be extremely valuable to us. We ended by leaving behind one thing after another, including the portable kitchen gardens Beaver had invented. After a day of dismal hesitation, he burst out laughing and declared that they were "stupid contraptions that would only have given us grief." He hesitated longer over the respiratory devices and the self-heated clothing. Finally, we decided to leave them, too, even if it meant coming back to get them for a new attempt if necessary. We left all these objects behind in the care of our crewmen, who would transport them to the yacht where the four men would settle in after our departure, leaving the house free for new arrivals.

The question of the respiratory devices had been heatedly debated among us. Should we count on bottled oxygen or acclimatization for tackling high altitudes? Recent expeditions in the Himalayas had not solved the problem, in spite of the brilliant success achieved by the partisans of acclimatization. Besides, our devices were much more refined than the equipment used on those expeditions. They were not only much lighter, but should have been more efficient as well, because they provided the mountaineer not with pure oxygen but a carefully dosed mixture of oxygen and carbon dioxide; the presence of this gas, stimulating to the respiratory centers, should have allowed a considerable reduction in the amount of oxygen required. But as we reflected on the problem and gathered information on the nature of the mountains we would have to climb, it became increasingly clear that our expedition would be long, very long; it would surely take years. Our oxygen supplies would not be sufficient, and we had no means of recharging them up there. Sooner or later, we would have to leave them behind, and better to do it right away so as not to delay the acclimatization process. We were assured, besides, that the only way to survive in the higher regions of these mountains was to become progressively accustomed to the altitude, and we were told that the human organism modifies and adapts itself to an extent that we could not yet imagine.

On the advice of our head porter, we exchanged our skis, which he told us would hamper us on uneven terrain, for a species of narrow snowshoes, which were pliable and covered with the skin of a kind of marmot. They make it easier to walk in wet snow, of course, but also to slide quickly down the slopes in a descent; folded up they fit easily into our rucksacks. We wore our climbing shoes to start out, but took along the native moccasins made of "tree leather," a kind of bark which, when worked, resembles cork and rubber, to wear later. This substance holds the heat in very well, and as it is encrusted with silica, it adheres to ice almost as well as to rocks. We could then dispense with crampons, which are so dangerous at the very highest altitudes because their straps, binding the feet, reduce the circulation of the blood and encourage frostbite. On the other hand, we kept our ice axes, excellent tools that from now on could hardly be more refined than the scythe, for example, as well as our picks, our silk ropes, and a few very simple pocket instruments: compasses, altimeters, and thermometers.

We were grateful, after all, for the rain that allowed us to make so many useful adjustments to our gear. We walked a great deal each day under the downpour to gather information, provisions, and various supplies. And thanks to this our legs got used to functioning again after our long voyage.

It was during these rainy days that we began to call each other by our first names. This was primed by our established custom of saying "Hans" and "Karl," and this small change was not a simple effect of intimacy. If we now called each other Judith, Renée (my wife), Pierre, Arthur, Ivan, and Theodore (my first name), it had another meaning for each of us. We were beginning to shed our old personalities. Just as we were leaving our encumbering equipment on the coast, we were also preparing to leave behind the artist, the inventor, the doctor, the scholar, the literary man. Beneath their old disguises, men and women were already peaking out. Once more, Pierre Sogol set us an example—without knowing it, and without suspecting that he was becoming a poet. He told us one evening, when we gathered for a meeting on the beach with the head porter and the donkey-driver:

"I have led you here, and I have been your leader. Here I relinquish my general's helmet, which was a crown of thorns for the image I had of myself. In the untroubled depths of my memory of myself, a little child is awakening and makes the old man's mask sob. A little child who is searching for a father and mother, who is searching with you for help and protection; protection from his pleasure and his dreams, and help to become what he is without imitating anyone."

As he spoke, Pierre had been digging in the sand with the end of his stick. Suddenly he stared, crouched down, and picked something up—something that shone like a tiny dewdrop. It was a peradam, a very small one, but his first peradam and ours. The head porter and the donkey driver grew pale and opened their eyes wide. Both of them were old men who had tried the ascent and been discouraged over the matter of currency.

"Never," said the first, "never in human memory has one been found so far down! On the shore itself! Perhaps it's just luck. But perhaps we are being given a new sign of hope? To set off once again?"

A hope, which he had thought dead, burned anew in his heart.

One day the porter would take to the road again. The donkey-driver's eyes shone, too, but with envy.

"Luck," he said, "Pure luck! No one will get me up there again!"

Judith said, "We should all make ourselves some little pouches to wear around our necks for carrying the peradams we'll find."

This was indeed an indispensable foresight. The rain had stopped the evening before, the sun had begun to dry the trails. We were determined to leave the following day at dawn. This was our last preparation before going to bed: each of us, with great care, manufactured a pouch for the peradams to come.

CHAPTER 5

The night was still settled around us at the base of the fir trees, whose tops traced their high scrim on the pearl-colored sky. Then, low between the trunks, a reddish glow caught fire and several of us saw the sky opening to the faded blue of our grandmothers' eyes. Little by little the spectrum of greens emerged from the black, and now and then the fragrance of a beech tree refreshed the odor of resin and enhanced the scent of mushrooms. With the voices of rattles, brooks, silvery chimes, and flutes, the birds exchanged their morning greetings. We went on in silence. The caravan was long, with our ten donkeys, the three men leading them, and our fifteen porters. Each of us carried his portion of provisions for the day and his personal belongings. Some of us had rather heavy personal baggage to carry in our hearts, and in our minds as well. We had quickly recovered our mountaineer's slow, steady stride appropriate at the outset if you want to go a long distance without tiring. While walking, I went over in my mind the events that had led me there—from my article in the *Revue des Fossiles* and my first meeting with Sogol. The donkeys were, happily, trained not to walk too fast; they reminded me of the donkeys in Bigorre, and I found strength in watching the supple play of their muscles unbroken by useless contractions. I thought of the four quitters who had excused themselves from accompanying us. How far away they were, Julie Bonasse, Emile Gorge, Cicoria, and the good Alphonse Camard with his hiking songs! As if mountaineers ever sing as they walk. Yes, we sing once in a while, after a few hours of climbing over fallen rocks or hiking on the turf, but each man for himself, clenching his teeth. I, for example, sang: "tyak, tyak, tyak, tyak" —one "tyak" per step; on the snow, at high noon, this became: "tyak, chi chi tyak!" Someone else might sing: "stoom, di di stoom!" or: "gee . . . pof!" This is the only kind of mountaineers' hiking song I know.

We could no longer see the snowy summits but only wooded slopes interspersed with limestone cliffs, and the rushing torrent at the bottom of the valley to the right, through the clearings in the forest. At the last turn of the path, the marine horizon, which had continued to rise with us, had disappeared. I munched a piece of biscuit. The donkey's tail chased a cloud of flies into my face. My companions were also pensive. All the same, there was something mysterious in the ease with which we had reached the continent of Mount Analogue; and then, we seem to have been expected. I supposed it would all be explained later. Bernard, the head porter, was as pensive as we were, but less often distracted. It is true that our attention was constantly captured by a blue squirrel or a red-eyed ermine standing like a column in the middle of an emerald clearing splashed with orange agaric, or by a herd of unicorns, which we had first taken for chamois, that leaped across a treeless outcropping on the other side, or the flying lizard that hurled itself ahead of us from one tree to the next, its teeth chattering. Except for Bernard, all the men we had hired carried in their packs a small horn bow and a bundle of short, featherless arrows. At the first significant halt, a little before noon, three or four of them went off and came back with several partridges and a kind of big

Indian pig. One said to me: "We should take advantage while hunting is allowed. We will eat them this evening. Higher up, no more game!"

The path left the forest and descended by brightly sunlit clearings to the rushing torrent that sped along, surging loudly as we forded it. We raised clouds of iridescent butterflies from the humid bank, then began a long trek across exposed stones. We came back to the right bank, where an airy larch forest began. I was sweating, and I was singing my hiking song. We seemed to grow more and more pensive, but in fact we were less and less. Our path climbed over a high rocky ridge and turned to the right, where the valley narrowed into a deep gorge, then pitilessly twisted through a steep scrub of junipers and rhododendrons. We arrived at last in a mountain pasture drenched with countless streams where small, plump cows were grazing. Twenty minutes' walk through the soaking grass brought us to a rocky plateau shaded by small junipers, where we found several structures of dry stone crudely covered with branches; this was our first staging area. We still had two or three hours of daylight ahead of us to settle in. One of the shelters was to serve as a storage space for the baggage, the other as a dormitory—there were planks and clean straw, and an oven made of large stones. A third shelter, to our great surprise, was a dairy: jars of milk, slabs of butter, runny cheeses seemed to be waiting for us. Was the place inhabited? Bernard's first concern had been to order our men to put down their bows and arrows in the corner of the dormitory that was reserved for such things, their slingshots too, for several of them were armed. Then he explained it to us:

"It was still inhabited this morning. Someone must always be here to tend the cows. Besides, it is a law that they will explain to you up there: no camp must ever remain unoccupied for more than a day. The previous caravan probably left one or two men here and is awaiting our arrival to go on. They saw us coming from a distance and left immediately. We'll let them know we've arrived, and at the same time I'll show you where the trail up the Base begins."

We followed him for several minutes along a wide, rocky ledge to a platform that allowed us to see the head of the valley. It was a kind of irregular oval, into which the gorge emptied out, surrounded by the high rock walls of the summit from which, here and there, hung the tongues of glaciers. Bernard lit a fire, threw on some damp grass, then looked attentively in the direction of the oval. At the end of a few minutes, from a great distance, came an answering signal, a thin white plume of smoke hardly distinguishable from the slow mist of the waterfalls.

Man becomes highly alert in the mountains to any sign indicating the presence of his peers. But this distant smoke was particularly moving to us, this greeting addressed to us by strangers climbing ahead of us on the same path. For from now on the path linked our fate to theirs, even if we should never meet. Bernard knew nothing about them.

From where we stood we could follow with our eyes nearly half the second day's journey. We had decided to take advantage of the fine weather and leave the following morning. Perhaps we would be lucky enough to find our guide at the Base that very day; but perhaps, too, we would have to wait for his return from another trip, long or short. The eight of us would leave with all the porters but two, who would stay behind to tend the cows, while the donkeys and their drivers would descend once more to take on new supplies. We calculated that in eight trips the donkeys could transport all the necessary provisions and clothing from the house on the coast to Prés-mouillés (Damp-Meadow)—the name of the first staging area. During this time, we would shuttle back and forth with the porters between Prés-mouillés and the Base; we would have to make at least thirty trips, with supplies weighing ten to fifteen kilos. Taking into account the likelihood of some bad weather, this would take us at least two months, and we would thus have accumulated at the Base enough to subsist for two years. But two months of cow pastures!—

the younger members of the expedition were a little impatient at the prospect.

We could scarcely talk up there on our platform because of a high and powerful waterfall that thundered down a few hundred meters away. A footbridge, if one can call it that, made of three or four cables strung from one bank to the other, spanned the gorge where the waterfall rushed. We would have to cross it tomorrow morning. Just before the waterfall stood a kind of tall cairn surmounted by a cross—a wayside cross or burial mound. Bernard looked in that direction with a strangely grave expression. Then he abruptly pulled himself away from his thoughts and made us return to the refuge, where the porters should have prepared the meal. Indeed they had, and thanks to their ingenious management we scarcely had to touch our provisions. They had gathered excellent mushrooms along the way, and cut various species of thistle buds, all extremely good raw or boiled. And the game was much appreciated by all, except for Bernard, who would not touch it. We had also noticed that he made sure no one had moved the bows and other weapons since our arrival. But it was only after the meal—at sunset, which lit the wooded summits downstream with glorious color—only then, while everyone was digesting around the fire and asked him about the monument we had noticed near the great waterfall, that he opened up to us.

"It's my brother," he said. "I must tell you his story because we may be together a long time, and you should know what kind of man (he spat into the fire) you are dealing with.

"My men are such children! They complain that hunting is strictly forbidden from here on up. There is plenty of game in the area, sure! But the guides know what they're doing up there, forbidding hunting beyond Prés-mouillés. They have their reasons, and I should know. For a rat that I killed less than fifty steps from here, I lost the four peradams that I had taken such trouble to find and keep, and I lost ten years of my life.

"I come from a peasant family settled at Port-des-Singes for centuries. Several of my ancestors left for the mountains and became guides. But my parents, afraid to see me leave as well—I was their oldest son—did everything they could to keep me from answering the call of the mountains. To this end they pushed me to marry very young. Down below I have a wife whom I love and a grown son; he could do the climb now, and she could too. After my parents' death— I was thirty-five years old—I suddenly saw the emptiness of my life. What then? Would I, too, go on raising my son so that he in turn would perpetuate the line, and so on? What for? I am not very good at expressing myself, you see, and at that time I was even less so. But I felt squeezed by the throat. One day I met a high altitude guide, in transit at Port-des-Singes, who had come to buy provisions from me. I pounced on him, shook him by the shoulders, and I could only shout at him: 'why, why?'

"He answered me gravely: 'It's true. But now you should think: 'how?' He spoke to me at length that day and the days following. At last he gave me a date for the next spring—it was autumn then—at the chalets of the Base, where he would form a caravan in which he would include me. I was able to convince my brother to come with me. He, too, wanted to know why, and wanted to leave the confines of the lower regions behind.

"Our caravan of twelve people worked well and managed to settle in at the first camp for the winter. Spring came again, and I decided to go back down to Port-des-Singes to see my wife and my son in the hope of preparing them to accompany me. Between the chalets of the Base and this place where we are, I was caught in a terrifying torment of wind and snow that lasted three days. The trail was cut in twenty places by avalanches. I had to bivouac two nights running without sufficient food and fuel. When the weather cleared, I was a hundred paces from here. I stopped, exhausted with hunger and fatigue. At this period, the livestock had not yet climbed as far as Prés-mouillés; I would have found nothing to eat there. Then, on the slope of fallen rocks in front of me, I saw an old rock rat come out of his hole. This animal is something like a cross between a field mouse and a marmot. He was coming to warm himself in the first rays of the sun. With a well flung stone I hit his head, fetched him, cooked him on a fire of rhododendrons, and devoured the tough meat. With regained strength I slept an hour or two, then I hastened down to Port-des-Singes, where my wife, my son, and I celebrated our reunion after such a long absence. I could not, however, persuade them to come back up with me again that year.

"One month later, as I was about to take the mountain trail again, I was called before a tribunal of guides to answer for the murder of that old rat. How they had learned about the business I don't know. The law is inflexible: I was forbidden access to the mountains above Prés-mouillés for three years. After these three years I could ask to leave again with the first caravan on the condition, however, that I repair the damage my act may have caused. It was a hard blow. I was forced to take up my life once more, temporarily, at Port-des-Singes. With my brother and my son I devoted myself to agriculture and animal husbandry in order to furnish provisions for the caravans. We also organized companies of porters whose services could be hired as far as the forbidden zone. Thus, while earning our living, we retained our connection with the mountain people. Soon, my brother, too, was eaten up with the desire to leave, with that need for the heights that gets into your blood like a poison. But he decided he would not leave without me and wanted to wait for my sentence to expire.

"At last the day came! I proudly carried with me in a cage a fat rock rat whom I'd easily captured and would free as I passed the place where I had killed the other one—since I had to 'repair the damage.' Alas, the extent of the damage was only about to be revealed. As we were leaving Prés-mouillés, at sunrise, a terrifying noise rang out. The entire slope of the mountain, which was not yet cut through by the great waterfall, crumbled, burst, exploded into an avalanche of stones and mud. A cataract of water carrying blocks of ice and rock fell from the tongue of the glacier that dominated this slope, and hollowed out huge gullies in the flank of the mountain. A good part of the trail, which at that time climbed from Prés-mouillés and crossed the slope much higher up, was destroyed. For several days, rock slides, gushes of water and mud, and earth slides kept coming, one after the other, and blocked our way. The caravan returned below, to Port-des-Singes, in order to equip itself for unforeseen dangers, then set out in search of a new trail toward the chalets of the Base along the other bank—a very long, risky, and difficult path on which several men perished. I was forbidden to leave until a commission of guides had determined the causes of the catastrophe. At the end of a week, I was called before this commission, which declared that I was responsible for the disaster, and that by virtue of the first judgment I would have to repair the damage.

"I was flabbergasted. But they explained to me how things had transpired, according to the commission's findings. Here is what was explained to me—impartially, objectively, and today I would even say kindly, but in a categorical fashion. The old rat I had killed fed chiefly on a species of wasp found abundantly in this place. But, especially at his age, a rock rat is not agile enough to catch wasps in flight; so he usually ate only the sick and the weak who dragged themselves on the ground and could barely fly. In this way he destroyed the wasps that carried defects or germs that, through heredity or contagion, would have spread dangerous illnesses in the colonies of these insects without his unconscious intervention. Once the rat was dead, these illnesses spread quickly, and by the following spring there were hardly any wasps left in the region. These wasps, gathering nectar from the flowers, ensured their pollination. Without them, a great many plants that played an important role in stabilizing the shifting earth,

Note from the French Edition

According to René Daumal's last outlines and working notes, *Le Mont Analogue* was to contain seven chapters. We have chosen to publish the two key documents rather than a hypothetical but possible reconstruction of the missing part of the narrative.

The first involves chapter 5. It gives us a glimpse of the end of the story of Bernard, the head porter, and indicates the two themes still to be dealt with: "sending provisions to the previous caravan" and "the language of the guides."

The second contains the material for chapter 6—which would have dealt with the "other expedition" of Alphonse Camard, Emile Gorge, Julie Bonasse, Benito Cicoria, which could only end in disaster—and of chapter 7, in which Daumal would most likely have addressed the reader directly.

Between 1938 and 1941-1942, René Daumal wrote several other texts along with *Le Mont Analogue* which are very important for understanding the meaning of this "novel." We offer them here in chronological order.

The first is the beginning of a "treatise of analogical alpinism," conceived well before the writing of *Le Mont Analogue*. The second is comprised of two paragraphs of introduction which do not sum up

overnight stop
at the first refuge

cabins at the base
setting up the first camp
first exercises
guides' advice
accident

ermine
unicorns

good-byes
to the crew
the sea's horizon behind us
showed – the dawn

while walking . . .
reflections (mystery of so easy an arrival)
songs (tyak! tyak!)

hunting (prohibited higher up: ecological balance)
head porter's story (hunts – has to pay back – gets discouraged)
hunted for 3 years

rat
Base Camp   bees
plants
landslides
rocks   bridge
ice pocket . . .   *?cards?*

need to send supplies to the preceding group
?homing pigeons?

the sun burns!
– 'clouds'
guides' language

V –
conseils des guides : connus, mais sens nouveau
guides – degrés : 7 ou 49 ou 8 ou 10 ou 50 ..
Langue.
invités au 2e camp, par petits groupes, par le guide n° 2 – de là, par la
"lunette décourbeuse", observons...
VI – L'autre expédition
récit de Julie Bonasse, rescapée (?)
(2 Petit Informé
"et vous alors ?"
que cherchez-vous ?
VII

how the story began but allow the reader to enter into it, and two paragraphs which, in the guise of a conclusion, show how René Daumal planned to "clothe this truthful story to make it believable."

These four paragraphs serve to frame chapter 1, published in *Mesures* (#1, 15 January 1940).

The third and fourth texts concern chapter 3 and were meant to introduce the "Tale of the Hollow-men and the Bitter-Rose" (which was published in *Cahiers du Sud*, #239, October 1941).

1

Forward—My observations are those of a beginner. As they are completely fresh in my mind and concern the first difficulties a beginner encounters, they may be more useful to beginners making their first ascents than treatises written by professionals. These are no doubt more methodical and complete, but are intelligible only after a little preliminary experience. The entire aim of these notes is to help the beginner acquire this preliminary experience a little faster.

Definitions—*Alpinism* is the art of climbing mountains by confronting the greatest dangers with the greatest prudence.

Art is used here to mean the accomplishment of knowledge in action.

You cannot always stay on the summits. You have to come down again . . .

So what's the point? Only this: what is above knows what is below, what is below does not know what is above. While climbing, take note of all the difficulties along your path. During the descent, you will no longer see them, but you will know that they are there if you have observed carefully.

There is an art to finding your way in the lower regions by the memory of what you have seen when you were higher up. When you can no longer see, you can at least still know.

I questioned him: "What do you mean when you talk about 'analogical alpinism'?

"It's the art of . . ."

"What is an art?"

"The value of danger:

temerity—suicide.

Short of that, no satisfaction."

"What is danger?"

"What is prudence?"

"What is a mountain?"

Keep your eyes fixed on the way to the top, but don't forget to look at your feet. The last step depends on the first. Don't think you have arrived jut because you see the peak. Watch your feet, be certain of your next step, but don't let this distract you from the *highest* goal. The first step depends on the last.

When you take off on your own, leave some trace of your passage that will guide your return: one rock set on top of another, some grass pierced by a stick. But if you come to a place you cannot cross or that is dangerous, remember that the trace you have left might lead the people following you into trouble. So go back the way you came and destroy any traces you have left. This is addressed to anyone who wants to leave traces of his passage in this world. And even without wanting to, we always leave traces. Answer to your fellow men for the traces you leave behind.

Never stop on a crumbling slope. Even if you believe your feet are firmly planted, while you take a breath and looking at the sky the earth is gradually piling up under your feet, the gravel is slipping imperceptibly, and suddenly you are launched like a ship. The mountain always lies in wait for the chance to trip you up.

If, after climbing up and down three times through gullies that end in sheer drops (visible only at the last moment), your legs begin to tremble from knee to heel and your teeth start to chatter, first reach a little platform where you can stop safely; then, remember all the curse words you know and hurl them at the mountain, and spit on the mountain; finally, insult it in every way possible, swallow some water, have a bite to eat, and start climbing again, calmly, slowly, as if you had your whole lifetime to undo this bad move. In the evening, before going to sleep, when it all comes back to you, you will see then that it was just a performance. It wasn't the mountain you were talking to, it wasn't the mountain you conquered. The mountain is only rock or ice, with no ears or heart. But this performance may have saved your life.

Besides, in difficult moments you'll often surprise yourself talking to the mountain, sometimes flattering it, sometimes insulting it, sometimes promising, sometimes threatening. And you'll imagine that the mountain answers, as if you had said the right words by speaking gently, by humbling yourself. Don't despise yourself for this, don't feel ashamed of behaving like those men our social scientists call primitives and animists. Just keep in mind when you recall these moments later that your dialogue with nature was only the outward image of a dialogue with yourself.

Shoes are not like feet—we are not born with them. Therefore we can choose them. Let yourself be guided in this choice first by experienced people, then by your own experience. Very quickly you will be so used to your shoes that every nail will seem like a finger, capable of testing the rock and gripping it firmly; they will become a sensitive and reliable tool, like a part of yourself. And yet you were not born with them; and yet, when they wear out, you will throw them away and remain what you are.

Your life somewhat depends on your footwear. Care for them properly, but a quarter of an hour per day will be plenty, for your life depends on several other things as well.

A climber far more experienced than I told me, "When your feet will no longer carry you, you have to walk with your head." And that's true. It is not, perhaps, in the natural order of things, but isn't it better to walk with your head than to think with your feet, as often happens?

If you slip or have a minor spill, don't interrupt your momentum but even as you right yourself recover the rhythm of your walk. Take note of the circumstances of your fall, but don't allow your body to brood on the memory. The body always tries to make itself interesting by its shivers, its breathlessness, its palpitations, its shudders, sweats, and cramps. But it is very sensitive to its master's scorn and indifference. If it feels he is not fooled by its jeremiads, if it understands that enlisting his pity is a useless effort, then it falls back into line and compliantly accomplishes its task.

The moment of danger
The difference between panic and presence of mind
Automatism (master or servant)

2

I would have liked to tell you the whole story right now. But since this would be too long, here is the beginning. Perhaps it is always artificial to speak of the beginning and the end of a story, since we always grasp only the intermediate phases. But at the source of the events there was a meeting, and every meeting is a relative beginning, and this meeting in particular is a whole story in itself.

What I have to tell is so extraordinary that I must take certain precautions. To teach anatomy, one uses conventional diagrams—rather than photographs—which differ in every respect from the object to be studied, except that certain relations—specifically, those that form the *thing to be known*—are preserved. I have done the same here.

This is how the project for an expedition to Mount Analogue came into being. Now that I have begun, I should tell you the sequel: how it was proved that a continent hitherto unknown, with mountains much higher than the Himalayas, existed on our Earth; how no one had noticed it before; how we reached it; what beings we met there; how another expedition, for other purposes, nearly perished in the most ghastly way; how little by little we began to put down roots, so to speak, in this new world; and how, nonetheless, the journey has scarcely begun . . .

Very high and very far up in the sky, above and beyond the successive circles of increasingly elevated peaks, of increasingly white snow, so dazzling the eye cannot bear it, invisible due to excessive light, stands the extreme point of Mount Analogue. "There, at the summit sharper than the sharpest needle, alone stands he who fills all space. Up there, in the finer air where all is frozen, there alone exists the crystal of ultimate stability. Up there, in the full fire of the sky where all burns, there alone exists perpetual incandescence. There, at the center of all, is he who sees each thing done in its beginning and its end." This is what the mountain men sing here. This exists. "You say that this exists, but if it's a little cold your heart is transformed into a mole; if it's a little warm, your head is filled with a cloud of flies; if you're hungry, your body becomes a donkey heedless to the cudgel; if you're tired, your feet know how to stall!" This is another song the mountain men are singing as I write, as I try to figure out how to craft this truthful tale to make it believable.

3

All sorts of voices again made themselves heard. I could pick and choose among the things they said. One spoke of the man who, having come down from the peaks, found himself below once more, where his gaze encompassed no more than the immediate surroundings. "But he has the memory of what he saw, which can still guide him. When one can no longer see, one can still know; and one can bear witness to what one has seen." Another spoke of shoes, and said how each nail, each wing-nail becomes as sensitive as a finger that tests the terrain and firmly grips the slightest rough patch. "And yet these are only shoes, we are not born with them, and a quarter of an hour of care each day is enough to keep them in good repair. While feet we are born with, and we will die with them—at least so we think. But are we really sure? Are there not feet that survive their owner, or that die before him?" (I shut this one up, it was becoming eschatological.) Another spoke of Olympus and of Golgotha, another of polyglobuli and the peculiarities of the mountain men's metabolism. Another finally announced that "we were wrong to claim that the high mountains were poor in legends, and that it knew at least one quite noteworthy example." He specified that, truthfully, in this legend the mountains served as a setting more than a symbol, and that the true site of the story was "at the junction of our humanity and a superior civilization, where an established truth is perpetuated." Quite intrigued, I begged him to tell me the story. Here it is. I listened to it and I try to reproduce it with all the attention and precision I am capable of—which means that what you find here is merely a rather pale and approximate translation.

4

On a certain day in a certain August, I was coming down from the bitter and hard, snow-covered regions, where gusts of hail blow and storms begin. I knew that various circumstances would soon prevent me from returning to the aerial land of wind-torn ridges dancing in the middle of the sky, the illusion from above and below of the white coastal paths traced in the blue-black abyss from above, which collapsed in the midst of a silent afternoon, among the slopes seamed with gullies and shimmering with black ice, where sulfurous explosions begin. Once more I had wanted to inhale the greenish breath of a crevasse, run my fingers over a stone slab, slip between crumbling blocks, rope together a group of climbers, weigh the back-and-forth of a gust of wind, listen to the steel chime on the ice and the small, crystalline fragments hurtle into the trap of the deceptive *rimaye*—a killing machine powdered and draped with gems; I wanted to trace a trail in the diamonds and dust, entrust myself to two strands of hemp, and eat prunes while suspended in space. Crossing through a cloud cover on my descent, I had stopped at the first saxifrage, before a great fall of seracs, a gigantic sash of iridescent folds that descended in spirals toward the great desert of stones at the bottom.

For a long time now I had had to stay below, lying down or gathering flowers, my pickax under a chest. Then I remembered that I was a man of letters by profession. And that I had a splendid opportunity to use this profession for its usual purpose, which is to speak instead of doing. Being unable to go mountain climbing, I would sing about the mountain climbers from below. I must admit that this was my intention. But fortunately, it released a revolting odor inside me: the odor of that literature which is merely a dead end, the odor of words that we cast instead of acting, or to console ourselves for being unable to do so.

I began to think more seriously, with the heavy clumsiness required to mull something over, just as one conquers one's body by conquering rock and ice. I would not speak *of* the mountain but *through* the mountain. With this mountain as language, I would speak of another mountain, which is the way that joins earth and sky, and I would speak of it not to resign myself but to exhort myself.

And the whole story—my story until today, clothed in mountain words—was traced before me. A whole story that I now need the time to tell, and also time to finish living.[1]

I was leaving with a group of friends to seek the Mountain which is the path joining Earth and Sky. It *must* exist somewhere on our planet, and must be the dwelling of a superior humanity. This was proven rationally by the man we called Father Sogol, our senior in mountain matters and the leader of the expedition.

And now we have reached the unknown continent, seed of superior substances implanted in the terrestrial crust, protected from curious and covetous gazes by the curvature of its space—just as a drop of mercury, by its surface tension, remains impenetrable to the finger that tries to touch its center. By our calculations—thinking of nothing else—by our desires—abandoning all other hope—by our efforts—renouncing all comfort—we had forcibly entered this new world. So it seemed to us. But later we knew that if we had been able to reach the foot of Mount Analogue, it was because the invisible doors of this invisible country had been open to us by those who guard them. The cock crowing in the milk of dawn believes that his song

1. This story is the subject of a book in progress, *Mont Analogue*, which includes in part the pages that follow.

makes the sun rise; the child howling in a closed room thinks his cries make the door open. But the sun and the mother follow courses set by the laws of their beings. Those who see us even if we cannot see ourselves, answer our puerile calculations, our fickle desires, our small and awkward efforts with a generous welcome.

Afterword

And so René Daumal stopped mid-sentence in the fifth chapter of *Mount Analogue*. His customary graciousness would not allow him to keep the visitor waiting who was knocking at his door on that day in April, 1944. It was the last day that Daumal could still hold his pen.

His close friend, A. Rolland de Renéville, who was aware of Daumal's failing condition and foresaw that he would not be able to finish *Mount Analogue*, had the idea of asking him to sketch out how future episodes of the work should unfold. He used the pretext that his wife, Cassilda, who had read what was already written, was impatient to know the end of the adventure. With his usual mix of seriousness and humor, René Daumal summarized his intentions in a few words; those words are engraved on my memory.

"In the course of the fifth and sixth chapters, I plan to describe the expedition of the four quitters. You remember that the cast of characters initially included Julie Bonasse, the Belgian actress; Benito Cicoria, the ladies' tailor; Emile Gorge, the journalist; and Alphonse Camard, the prolific poet—all of whom left us even before we started out. However, one day they finally decided to embark on their own with some of their friends to discover Mount Analogue, for they were convinced that we had tricked them; if we had gone in search of the famous Mountain, it must have been to find more than a superior type of humanity. That's why they called us "the jokers." They thought that this mountain must contain oil, gold, and other earthly riches and must be jealously guarded by a people who would not hand anything over without a fight. As a result, they equipped themselves with a warship armed with the most powerful modern weapons, then weighed anchor. Their voyage involved many a twist and turn, but at last they arrived in sight of Mount Analogue and prepared to make use of their weapons. However, because they were ignorant of the basic laws of the place, they were helplessly caught in a whirlpool. Condemned to turn around and around, they were still able to bombard the coast, but all their projectiles came back to them like boomerangs, so their fate was ludicrous."

We can imagine the inventive and humorously profound tale René Daumal would have told us recounting the misadventures of these misguided seekers, who had occasion to glimpse "the mountain that is the way uniting Heaven and Earth" but could not understand its nature or imagine how to approach it.

Daumal continued by sketching what he meant to show in the final chapter of his book:

"In the end, I want to focus at length on one of the laws of Mount Analogue: to reach the summit, one must go from camp to camp. But before leaving a camp, one must prepare those who are coming to occupy the place one leaves behind. Only after preparing them can one climb higher. That is why, before dashing off to a new camp, we had to go back down to teach our new knowledge to other seekers . . ."

It is very likely that René Daumal would have explained what he meant by this work of preparation. The fact is that in his own life he was working hard to prepare many minds for the difficult voyage toward Mount Analogue.

The title of his last chapter was to be:

And you, what are you looking for?

It is a better, more disturbing, and more productive question than the numerous pat answers usually made to it, a question, finally, that we must all answer for ourselves. Considering it seriously involves tapping into the deepest part of ourselves and cruelly, lucidly, listening to the sound it makes.

At the end of his life, René Daumal, though only on the threshold of his own research, had already made out whether the sound was full or empty. One would like to know more about it, to know the path he was taking even if he was interrupted—especially because he was interrupted.

The indicator has been given, nonetheless, condensed in precise terms in one of the last letters he wrote me, saying:

"Here is how I have summarized for myself what I would like those who work here with me to understand:

"I am dead because I have no desire,
I have no desire because I think I possess,
I think I possess because I do not try to give;
Trying to give, we see that we have nothing,
Seeing that we have nothing, we try to give ourselves,
Trying to give ourselves, we see that we *are* nothing,
Seeing that we are nothing, we desire to become,
Desiring to become, we live."

—VÉRA DAUMAL

More Tusk Books Published by
The Overlook Press

GRINGOS by Charles Portis
The classic and wonderfully bizarre novel of an American expatriate living in Mexico.
978-1-58567-093-2

HASH translated by Tom Geddes, Torgny Lindgren
The wittily bleak, startlingly original, elegantly crafted tale of an unlikely quest for the ultimate hash.
978-1-58567-651-4

THE HERETIC by Miguel Delibes
The World-renowned literary-historical novel that takes readers on a compelling journey through the Spanish Inquisition
978-1-58567-889-1

JILL by Philip Larkin
Larkin's novel of student life at Oxfod during World War II.
978-0-87951-961-2

JOB by Joseph Roth
An ageless novel about believing in miracles.
978-1-58567-374-2

THE LAST OF THE JUST by Andre Schwarz-Bart
A haunting novel of the Jewish experience.
978-1-58567-016-1

LEWI'S JOURNEY by Per Olov Enquist
A visionary epic novel of faith, sex, and intrigue from an author "in the front ranks of contemporary literary fiction" (Bruce Bawer, The New York Times Book Review).
978-1-58567-754-2

LOOKOUT CARTRIDGE by Joseph McElroy
A riveting novel rich with suspense and intrigue by the author rightly compared to Pynchon and Delillo.
978-1-58567-352-0

 The Overlook Press • Woodstock & New York • www.overlookpress.com

THE ROYAL PHYSICIAN'S VISIT by Per Olov Enquist
A tantalizing work of historical fiction by Sweden's premier literary novelist.
978-1-58567-196-0

THE SILENT PROPHET by Joseph Roth
The acclaimed writer's famous "Trotsky novel."
978-0-87951-384-9

A SMUGGLER'S BIBLE by Joseph McElroy
The legendary classic post-modern novel.
978-1-58567-351-3

STRAIT IS THE GATE by Andre Gide
The first novel of one of the twentieth century's most acclaimed voices—a
tragedy of passion and renunciation.
978-1-58567-605-7

TARABAS by Joseph Roth
The moving tale of a man caught in the coils of fate.
978-1-58567-328-5

THE TEMPEST by Juan M. de Prada
Prada's tempestuous, prize-winning novel set in Venice, Europe's quintessentially
enigmatic city.
978-1-58567-550-0

 The Overlook Press • Woodstock & New York • www.overlookpress.com

7/09- 3 - 17/08